PUFFIN BOOKS

Porterhouse Major

Editor: Kaye Webb

Rory had always wanted a really big pet, but his father was a dentist and animals might disturb the patients.

Then one day he had his brilliant idea – he wanted a St Bernard and, because his mother lectured on witchcraft, the house was full of books on magic, so why couldn't he make a spell to get what he wanted?

He was very busy in the surgery all afternoon, doing things with mistletoe berries, taking some salt from a packet of crisps, finding mouth-wash tablets and Simonsbath the skull. Then he went back to bed and awaited results. He was asleep when his sisters came home an hour later. 'Do wake up, we've something to show you!' said Joy, and there, sitting in a basket, was a tiny tabby kitten.

They fed him on minced Porterhouse steak and that was how he got his name. But Porterhouse the kitten wasn't tiny for long – soon he took up the whole sofa when he stretched out, and broke the springs when he jumped on and off, while his unusual cleverness and gift for conversation began to raise problems too ...

This really funny and original book is by Margaret J. Baker, whose other Puffin book, *Castaway Christmas*, was runner up for the Carnegie Medal in 1963. It is especially successful for 8 and 9 year olds.

Cover design by Shirley Hughes

Margaret J. Baker

Porterhouse Major

illustrated by
Shirley Hughes

Penguin Books

Penguin Books Ltd, Harmondsworth,
Middlesex, England
Penguin Books Australia Ltd, Ringwood,
Victoria, Australia

First published by Methuen 1967
Published in Puffin Books 1969

Made and printed in Great Britain by
Hazell Watson & Viney Ltd
Aylesbury, Bucks
Set in Linotype Granjon

Contents

1 The Arrival of Porterhouse

When Mr Cooper took over old Mr Prince's dental practice in Pebblesea, with his list of patients and the tall terrace house, his receptionist, Miss Needlepoint, was included – and Simonsbath.

A dentist had lived in the house ever since old Mr Prince's father had practised in the seaside town and visited his country patients in a dogcart. Everything in the house was arranged to serve the needs of the patients. The drawing-room, overlooking the long walled garden, had been turned into the surgery, and the dining-room became a waiting-room from nine-thirty in the morning till six o'clock every week-day. The table was piled with magazines and not a mustard-pot or toast crumb must be left to show.

Rory and Joy and Felicity had their play-room on the top floor of the house. From the windows looking past the Baptist Chapel, the pinnacled roof of the Railway Hotel, an orphanage, and Woolworths, they were just able to see the sea.

The house smelt of floor polish and fizzy mouth-wash tablets. On week-days it was hushed except for the grandfather clock ticking away the minutes in the hall, the telephone bell, and the muffled whirr of their father's drill. In the waiting-room the patients sat in silence. When Miss Needlepoint summoned them to the surgery they walked across the hall like aristocrats on their way to the guillotine, with short firm steps, not looking to right or left. The children knew they mustn't add to the patients' cares by making a noise or banging doors.

'All the same, living here is like boiling toffee in too small a saucepan,' Rory once remarked. 'However careful you are, sooner or later it boils over and takes ages to clean up.'

Rory's hair was the colour of fish-frying crumbs. His face was sprinkled with freckles. He was only eighteen months younger than his twin sisters but he was small for his age and often had colds.

'And how's your little brother?' patients would ask the twins when encountering them alone in the hall. 'What a shame he's in bed again. It's sad he should be so delicate.'

'Rory's not,' Felicity would declare, glancing uneasily up the stairs in case her brother had heard. 'It's only another of his beastly colds. Daddy says they're worse than all the plagues of Egypt, and Mummy only makes him stay in bed so that he doesn't sneeze over everybody else.'

Rory's bedroom was hung with pictures of shire carthorses, tusked mammoths and prehistoric monsters. His favourite hero was Goliath, who he thought had had almost as hard a time of it as the whale that had chosen to eat Jonah.

Being in bed so much gave Rory time to think. It was usually he who thought of the most interesting things to do. To brighten the time patients spent in the surgery Rory once purchased a goldfish to swim in the rinsing bowl beside the dental chair. He and the others had plugged up the outlet hole with modelling clay so that the fish would be comfortable. With water gushing into the bowl and the fish swimming round it had looked just like a real fountain. Their father had arrived while they were still admiring the effect, a second before the surgery was flooded. The goldfish still swam in the pool they had made specially at the far end of the garden.

With his ginger hair Rory's name fitted him better than those chosen for Joy and Felicity. The twins' names had happened by mistake. The curate, who was to christen them, had called in unexpectedly to have a tooth stopped only a few days after their birth.

'And what will you call your little twins?' he had asked after taking a long time to rinse away the rubble Mr Cooper had dislodged with his drill.

Mr Cooper smiled as he waited to resume his work. Even if the tooth was touchy the best thing was to finish the preparation of the cavity as soon as possible, but his patient's lips were firmly shut as he waited for an answer. Mr Cooper knew that the sooner he thought of two suitable names the sooner the curate would reopen his mouth. The trouble was that the twins, with their red faces and spikes of dark hair, had so far only been called Thump and Holler. They didn't look a bit like little girls who would one day need proper names at all. With his eyes on the curate and the drill raised in his hand Mr Cooper said the very first names which came into his head.

'Joy and Felicity from that prayer for the Queen in the morning service, and I only hope they'll live up to them.'

Ten years later the names still sat on the twins oddly like the best Sunday hats which always bobbed off their dark curly heads.

Miss Needlepoint had known all the children since they were babies but she still found them disturbing. The old days when only Mr Prince had lived in the house seemed like a golden dream.

'At least there are no pets,' Miss Needlepoint told her friend from the oculist's in the High Street, 'except of course for that goldfish in the garden. There was some talk of a budgerigar but I told Mrs Cooper I did not think it advisable. During surgery hours even the smallest noise can be disturbing.'

'Miss Needlepoint just fusses,' Joy declared when their receptionist had even objected to a couple of hamsters which would only wake up at night long after the last patient had departed. 'Daddy's far too interested in his work to be disturbed by anything, and I'm sure the patients don't really care so long as their teeth are put right.'

'Mummy hates not having animals in the house just as much as we do,' said Felicity. 'It's worse for her because at home in Ireland she had two wolf hounds besides her pointer and dozens of cats, but she says we mustn't annoy Miss Needlepoint because she's the finest receptionist Daddy's ever had.'

With her shingled grey hair, rimless spectacles, and nylon overall Miss Needlepoint was as much a part of the house as the gleaming plate on the front door and the ringing telephone. When Mr Cooper had finished a set of false teeth it was Miss Needlepoint who packed it into a stout cardboard box. Lying on a bed of cotton wool before she fastened down the lid, the denture seemed to glimmer up at her with the smile of the patient for whom it had been made.

In the surgery Miss Needlepoint mixed fillings on plates of thick clouded glass as carefully as a housewife would have mixed a pudding.

Under her management no one was ever late for an appointment. She despatched patients from the waiting-room to the surgery as swiftly as a sergeant would despatch his men for their first parachute drop from an aircraft.

In her spare time she embroidered cheerful mottoes to hang in the waiting room. 'Don't worry, it may never happen' was set above the printed list of National Health Charges, and another about helping others because the reader might never pass this way again took up the full length of the marble mantelshelf.

The children were far more frightened of Miss Needlepoint than they were of the other item which had been passed on from old Mr Prince's practice. Simonsbath was a very large man's skull which stood on the top of a corner cupboard in the surgery.

On Sunday afternoons their father often let Rory and his sisters play in the surgery. The chair, which would tilt backwards as well as go up and down, made a splendid seat for space travel. Sometimes their father gave them a drop of the quicksilver with which amalgam fillings were mixed. The tiny drop darted round in the palm of a hand like a mouse.

But it was the skull which interested them most of all.

'It must have belonged to someone,' Joy often remarked as she polished the smooth dome of the skull till it shone like ivory.

'Well, whoever that was must have been in Heaven for ages now,' said Felicity. 'He couldn't possibly want it any more.'

'And Daddy says there's no need to feel sorry for any man who had such a fine set of teeth as those,' said Rory. 'He couldn't have had a day's toothache in his whole life.'

Their only clue was a label fixed to the base of the skull. In the old dentist's faded handwriting were the words Simonsbath, June 1910, and Simonsbath was what the skull had always been called.

During the week their father was always busy. After his last appointment he usually went for a ride along the front before supper. He rode a racing bicycle, and however rough the weather he always returned cheerful and refreshed.

Their mother's hobby was very different. She lectured on folk-lore and magic. The books she needed to study looked almost as dull and heavy as their father's textbooks, but when she told Rory and his sisters fairy stories after tea in their upstairs sitting-room shivers ran up and down their backs. Her grown-up audiences felt the same. As she talked with a sheaf of typed notes in her hands it seemed as if in the stuffy hall a window had blown open. The dull dark curtains tugged on their rods and the leaves of oak and ash scattered the floor.

On a cold misted Monday in January at the beginning of the spring term Rory woke up with one of his worst colds. No one meant to be unkind but it couldn't have happened on a more unfortunate day.

'You look worse than any of the patients in *Dr Kildare* on television,' said Joy. 'Even the ones who don't get better but never really mind because he's looking after them.'

'Mummy heard you sneezing from the kitchen,' said Felicity. 'She told us to throw you a carton of paper handkerchiefs from the door without coming in. The stove's gone out so she can't come up. Breakfast's not even started yet and Daddy's just having cornflakes without sitting down. He has three emergency patients to fit in this morning and two impacted wisdom teeth to do down at the hospital after lunch.'

'And Mummy has to give a talk this afternoon,' added Joy. 'She's doing that one on wassailing, love potions and magic spells. A group meeting of the Women's Institute asked her specially, so unless you're really ill she doesn't want to miss it.'

'Of course I'm not,' said Rory from behind a large

paper handkerchief. 'I was just going to get up when you two came in. Now I'll have to hurry or I'll be late for school.'

'But Mummy said you weren't to go on any account,' said Felicity. 'She's rung them up already. She just wants you to stay in bed and keep warm.'

'It's much the best way,' said Joy, 'because if you do come down Daddy will only catch it. Then he'll have to cancel dozens of appointments and have to work twice as hard afterwards.'

'It's a horrid day so you're not missing much,' his mother told Rory half an hour later when she hurried up with his breakfast tray. 'You haven't a temperature and so long as you're sensible you'll probably be right as rain by tomorrow.'

The morning felt very long. Only Miss Needlepoint looked in at eleven.

'I told Mother I would pop up with your hot milk,' she said. 'I'm not a bit afraid of any tiresome little germs.'

'It's not a little germ,' said Rory; 'this one must be huge and perfectly horrid.'

'Dear me, we are down in the dumps,' said Miss Needlepoint briskly as she whisked back the curtains and shut off the bedside lamp. 'I really believe there's a big black dog right on your shoulder.'

'I wish there was,' said Rory with a sniff. 'The larger it was the more I would like it.'

'The very idea!' said Miss Needlepoint with a brisk smile that showed her front teeth, which were all still her own because she never ate sweets even at Christmas; and she hurried off.

Rory sat up in bed and wrote his last will and testament on the back of a jigsaw box. Distributing all his possessions always cheered him up. Even Miss Needlepoint would realize how much she had wronged him when she learnt that he had left her his three-colour torch, which only needed a new battery, an almost full book of trading stamps, and his goldfish, with enough money to keep it in ants' eggs for the rest of its life. Setting aside a large enough sum would use up most of his post office account, but Rory thought it would be worth it. Having a dumb creature to care for would be good for Miss Needlepoint, even if she did find it tiresome on frosty mornings to make sure the goldfish's pond hadn't frozen solid.

After the will was finished Rory sat thinking. Till Miss Needlepoint had mentioned the big black dog he had almost forgotten how much he wanted the company of some really large animal of his own. He pictured his hand resting lightly on the noble head of a St Bernard, or all the eyes of the crowd upon him as he rode into the unsaddling enclosure on the winner of the Derby or the Grand National.

But just wishing was no use. For what he wanted to happen his wishes needed far more help than wishbones or four-leaved clover could give. They needed something really scientific which had been used by past generations and found successful.

The idea came to him like a flash of electric sparks.

A jigsaw puzzle and two books landed on the floor as Rory jumped out of bed, slipped on his dressing-gown, and crept down the stairs to his parents' bedroom. As he had hoped, his mother's notes for the lecture she was to deliver that afternoon lay on her desk.

Rory's cold was forgotten as he searched through the pages until he found what he needed. Five minutes later he was back in bed frowning over the items in a hurriedly copied list. Rory knew that when he and his sisters cooked sweets they hardly ever had all the ingredients listed in the cookery book. Usually the sweets were just as eatable with some items left out or replaced by others. Today if he was to execute his plan he would have to do the same with many of the items on his list, but at least the most important was available in the house. All he needed was to dare to use it.

'You look so much better, Rory, I really think you might come downstairs this afternoon,' said his mother when she brought his lunch. 'It's a shame Daddy and I both have to be out, but Miss Needlepoint will be in her office if you need anything, and you'll be quite comfortable sitting by the fire.'

That afternoon Miss Needlepoint was busy in her office with a complicated form when Rory darted across the hall and opened the surgery door. The house was silent, but as Miss Needlepoint completed the form she looked up. Surely she had heard the well-oiled click of the surgery door as it was gently closed? She set down her pen and hurried down the hall.

In the surgery all was still. Only the sterilizer bubbled.

In the glass cabinet the instruments lay in neat rows just as she had left them. Above the chair the powerful light only glimmered like a clouded moon. The drill was hooked back like the beak of a giant bird.

Probably Mr Cooper had not shut the door properly and it had slammed to, Miss Needlepoint decided as the telephone rang in her office and she hurried back to answer it.

If the telephone had not summoned her when it did, she might have noticed that in the shadowed corner of the surgery a chair stood crooked as if it had been hurriedly pulled out from the wall, and that the top of the corner cupboard nearby was empty.

'Why, you are dark in here,' said Miss Needlepoint two hours later as she entered the sitting-room with a tea tray in her hands and switched on the light. 'I'm afraid it's been a long afternoon for you up here alone but I hope you weren't too dull.'

'Not a bit really,' said Rory. 'There was plenty to do.'

Rory sat bundled in his dressing-gown close to the fire in the big armchair.

'Well, as soon as you've had tea I should pop back to bed,' said Miss Needlepoint. 'You look just a little flushed.'

For once Rory didn't argue. As he trailed upstairs ten minutes later with a hot-water bottle, he felt as if he had travelled a long way and just come home, but what he had wanted to do was done. Now nothing was left except to see what came of it.

He was asleep when his sisters greeted him from the doorway an hour later.

'Do wake up, we've something to show you!' said Joy.

'Daddy found it left in one of the shelters on the front,' said Felicity, 'with nothing to eat but scraps of bread that were meant for the gulls.'

'He brought him home in the saddle-bag of his bicycle,' said Joy. 'Even Miss Needlepoint saw he couldn't leave him to starve, and the sea's really rough. One big wave breaking over the promenade might have washed him away altogether.'

Rory sat up in bed and blinked.

In her arms Felicity held an old shopping basket. Sitting in the basket, with his fur still spiked with spray and his head sunk on his chest, was a tabby kitten.

'His name is Porterhouse,' explained Felicity, 'because that's the sort of steak we gave him for supper, minced really small.'

'Daddy says he's tiny now but with really good food he'll grow quite large,' said Felicity.

'I'm sure he will,' said Rory. 'Now he's come today that's bound to happen.'

Even as he spoke, the kitten raised his head, and staring straight at Rory he began to purr so that the sound filled the room like the hum of bees on a summer day.

2 A Good Doer

'Rory watches Porterhouse grow just like Daddy watched that marrow he wanted for the Produce Show,' Felicity remarked a month later when she and Joy were cleaning their teeth in the bathroom with a new battery-operated brush their father wanted to test. 'He's weighed Porterhouse on Mummy's scales almost every day. He let me look at his weight card and since Porterhouse came he's gained over eight pounds. Rory didn't seem at all surprised but I'm sure no ordinary cat ought to grow that fast.'

Joy frowned as she screwed her own toothbrush head into the holder. In the garden Rory was playing with their new cat. Porterhouse looked very different from the bedraggled kitten her father had found abandoned in the shelter. His tabby fur shone as he skidded over the grass and captured a ball between his white tipped paws. With threshing tail he rolled on a flower bed and two wallflower plants bent under his weight.

'I don't believe Porterhouse is an ordinary cat,' said Joy. 'Yesterday in the kitchen when Rory asked Porterhouse if he had had enough dinner he answered him.'

'But that's crazy!' said Felicity. 'Everyone talks to

cats and dogs but they know perfectly well that they won't ever reply.'

'Porterhouse did,' insisted Joy looking straight at her sister with a froth of pink toothpaste still on her lips. 'He had just begun to wash his face and he stopped with his paw half licked. "Ample, thank you," he said, "though I must say a drop of milk would wash those sprats down very nicely." I had to listen really hard to make out the words from his ordinary purr. Mummy was washing up and she didn't notice, but I know Rory heard because he went straight to the refrigerator and gave Porterhouse all the top off the best Jersey milk.'

'Then we'll have to ask him what's happened,' said Felicity. 'I'm sure he knows more than we do. He's been strange about Porterhouse from the moment he arrived.'

Rory was doing his prep in the play-room after tea when the twins had their first chance to talk to him alone. Porterhouse sat before the gas fire with an old tennis ball squashed under one heavy paw. His long whiskers shone in the firelight. A large pie-dish, which had contained all that was left of their tea-time milk, stood empty at his side. Rory's transistor radio was tuned in to a chat for old people about knitting hot-water bottle covers and bedsocks. The speaker spoke in a special cheerful voice such as Miss Needlepoint might have used to a troublesome five year old.

'For goodness' sake switch that off,' said Felicity. 'Joy and I want to talk to you.'

'What about?' asked Rory without looking up from the map of Italy that he was tracing.

'Porterhouse,' said Felicity. 'Why he's growing so fast and why you seemed to expect it right from the start.'

'And if he can talk,' said Joy. 'Felicity wouldn't believe me when I told her I heard him yesterday but I know you heard him too.'

Rory's freckled face was set. Rounding the toe of Italy the point of his pencil cut through the tracing-paper and made a rough scribble right across the Strait of Messina.

'If it will put your sisters' minds at rest I think you might just as well tell them,' said Porterhouse placidly. 'I'm sure what has happened need go no farther than this room.'

The girls stared at Porterhouse who was contentedly kneading the hearth-rug. The tennis ball lay punched and bitten by his side. They knew it would never bounce again.

'Considering that your brother had to make do with what was to hand and had given his word to keep out of the draughts he did very well,' went on Porterhouse, glancing at Rory with affection. 'No doubt he's reluctant to boast, but there's no need at all for him not to tell you the full details.'

'Rory never minds boasting and of course he'll tell us,' said Felicity firmly. 'The sooner we know why you're getting larger and larger like an R.A.F. rescue raft that blows up by itself the better.'

'And it's mean not to have told us from the beginning,' said Joy. 'We've always done everything together before.'

'This time it was different,' said Rory. 'Daddy often says the end justifies the means, but it was the means you might not have liked.'

In the firelight his face was pale and his hair glowed like burning stubble. They knew he had been scared by what he had done and yet would never admit it.

'It was the day I had that beastly cold,' said Rory. 'Miss Needlepoint told me I had a big black dog on my shoulder because I was so cross. I told her I wished I had and that really began it all. I decided to wish for the biggest animal anyone could have indoors. I didn't care what it was so long as it was alive and large.'

'But just wishing is never any use,' objected Joy. 'What else did you do?'

'I borrowed Mummy's lecture notes. There were two whole pages full of spells which people really used ages ago. I had the Friar's Balsam saucepan in my room already and I decided to try one that afternoon.'

'But however did you find the right things to put in?' asked Felicity. 'Mummy's always said they're mostly horrid like moss scraped from tombstones at midnight, and bats' blood.'

'I just made do with what I had,' said Rory. 'I used mouth-wash tablets instead of the bats' blood and one of those meat-cubes which have twelve mouth-watering ingredients. I thought the heart and liver of a cock which had last crowed seven days after the new moon might be in just one of them. I put salt from a packet of crisps in as well, still done up in the blue paper, and those mistletoe berries we meant to plant on the apple tree. I had to leave out lots of other things but I hoped having the most important ingredient of all would make up for all the rest.'

'What was that?' asked Felicity with a shiver because she was afraid she knew already.

'Simonsbath from the surgery,' said Rory. 'Lots of the spells said crossed bones as well, but I thought the skull might be enough, especially as it was extra large.'

'But Daddy's always told us we're only to borrow it for scientific purposes,' said Felicity.

'This was scientific,' insisted Rory, 'just like any experiment you had to try out. I had to see if the spell would work or not. The Friar's Balsam splashed a bit because I sneezed just as I was circling the saucepan round Simonsbath for the seventh time, but it didn't show and the skull really needed a good polish. Even Miss Needlepoint doesn't have time to dust that top shelf.'

'And the spell did work beautifully,' said Joy. 'No one nicer could have come than Porterhouse.'

'Or grown faster,' said Rory, stroking the cat from his head to the tip of his bushy tail.

'You are all more than kind,' said Porterhouse. 'Even on a most moderate diet I am what I fancy is known as a good doer and I hope I shall give satisfaction.'

'Even if Rory is so pleased I hope Porterhouse won't grow much larger,' Felicity said to her sister when Rory left with Porterhouse to give him his supper. 'If he grows much more Miss Needlepoint's bound to fuss. Even now you can hear him thump when he goes downstairs.'

'Probably he's just grown very fast all at once and now he'll stop,' said Joy. 'Even the very biggest cats are never half as big as St Bernard dogs.'

But remembering the shadowed sitting-room and the fire-lit skull neither of them was sure.

Even Rory jumped when that evening at supper his father mentioned the skull.

'I know how you've all puzzled over that label on the skull in my surgery,' he said. 'Today I've solved the mystery. It's really so simple we might have guessed for ourselves. An old friend of Mr Prince came in this afternoon and happened to notice the skull on top of the cupboard. He told me he was with Mr Prince the day he found the skull at a village called Simonsbath on Exmoor.'

'Well, there's nothing so remarkable in that,' said Mrs Cooper with a smile.

'Of course not,' said their father; 'but that village is on the river and has that name because a man called Simon used to bathe there. The queer thing is that our skull was discovered in the very pool Simon used, and Mr Prince always thought it might have been his.'

Rory stared at his father.

'But how could he know?' he asked.

Mr Cooper took the backbone off his second kipper and buttered another piece of toast.

'Because of the skull's extraordinary size,' he said. 'You see this Simon was supposed to be a giant.'

3 Wider Still and Wider

Knowing for certain what had happened made them all feel better.

'It's like Granny in Ireland going straight to the outsize department for her clothes,' Joy remarked as they took Porterhouse down to the beach the next morning to play on the empty sands. 'She told me that once she had decided it was no use to try anywhere else she never fussed about being fat any more.'

Thinking of the ample tweed-clad figure of their Irish grandmother and her beaming smile made even Porterhouse seem less large. In her house an extra-long basset hound stretched before the big stone fireplace with two wolf hounds and an old black labrador called Derby Brights.

'It's a shame we can't write and tell her what Rory's done,' added Joy as they watched Porterhouse splash across the sand after a new and extra-large beach ball. 'She'd be much more pleased about that than if he had passed dozens of exams.'

At their side with the wind ruffling his ginger hair Rory flushed.

'Of course finding exactly the right skull was mostly luck,' he said. 'Even with Simonsbath I don't expect I could ever make it happen half so well again.'

'Or unhappen,' said Felicity with a frown. 'This morning I borrowed Mummy's Bible with those tables of weights and measures at the back, and I worked out exactly how tall Goliath really was. He must have been well over eleven feet, and if he had owned a giant cat to match, that would have been as big as a full grown bob-tailed sheep dog.'

At home the big cat's purr sounded throughout the quiet house. Beneath his tabby stripes Porterhouse's fur shone with a ginger glow, which seemed to warm the room in which he lay as if some new form of central heating had been installed.

Porterhouse was always pleased and never put out about anything.

'Your mother really shouldn't have had this sofa re-upholstered,' Porterhouse told the children as he stretched out along its full length. 'That dent at the end near the fire didn't matter and I liked those feathers that puffed through that slit in the cushion.'

'Mummy had to have it done,' Felicity told him. 'Just jumping on and off you had broken three of the springs. They've put in extra strong ones this time and upholstered it in twill which they keep specially for approved schools and battleships.'

'And when Mummy explained at the shop that it was you who had done all those tears on the arms,' added Joy, 'the man told her he'd never seen the like and even a lioness with her cubs couldn't have come up to it.'

Porterhouse flexed his claws modestly so that they sank deep into the new upholstery.

'Of course that is more than generous,' he said; 'though I trust in my own small way I always try to do my best.'

'He just doesn't understand that people don't always do things specially for him,' Felicity remarked. 'It was the same with that bird-table Mrs Clarence put in her guest-house garden next door. Porterhouse thought he ought to eat up all the scraps she put on it just to be polite. Even then he fussed because he couldn't manage the string of monkey-nuts and the coconut.'

Rory was silent. Only that morning Porterhouse had jumped on to his bed with milk still on his whiskers.

'You wouldn't find many houses where milk is provided upstairs before breakfast,' he had told him. 'But it's like your father to guess I'm always peckish first thing. My usual bowl would have been easier but I managed very well from the cream jug and there was a plastic cloth on the tray which won't need ironing.'

Rory had sat up in bed. Feathers puffed into the air as Porterhouse flexed his paws on the eider-down.

'That was the milk on Daddy's early-morning tea-tray which you took,' said Rory. 'Now there won't be any more till the milkman comes at eight. Since you came there's always been only just enough.'

Porterhouse had been moved but unruffled.

'And that is so like your parents,' he had declared. 'They would always share their last drop with one in need.'

They realized just how large Porterhouse had grown a few weeks later when they went in search of a basket in which Porterhouse could travel at Whitsun.

'He likes to come with us even if it's only on a picnic,' Rory explained to the shop assistant. 'But Daddy won't have him cramped. The Vet says he's bound to fill out a good deal yet. He's given us the address of a special wholesaler where we can buy cod liver oil in bulk and vitaminized wheat germ to tide him over between breakfast and lunch.'

'Then you'd better have a show-basket for toy dogs,' the assistant advised. She found them one with a foam-rubber cushion covered in tartan, and a wire door.

At home Porterhouse stared doubtfully at the basket.

'No doubt it will do very well for my brush and comb with just a few tins of cat food and possibly the tin-opener,' he said.

'But it's for you,' explained Felicity. 'You must try

and fold up like one of those snakes that fit into wooden eggs in really expensive Christmas crackers.'

Porterhouse did his best to oblige. He folded his paws right under his chest and held his breath while they fastened the lid. Even so his ears were flattened against the wire door, his whiskers poked through, and the sides of the basket bulged.

'There's nothing bigger,' the assistant declared when they took back the basket to change it. 'Cats don't come that large.'

'Porterhouse does,' said Rory.

They took a crate of tinned cat-food instead, with two catnip mice and a book meant for zookeepers about the transport and care of leopards, jaguars and panthers. The manager of the concert party on the pier, who had arrived in the town with an aching molar tooth, gave Mr Cooper a hamper in which theatrical costumes were usually packed for Porterhouse to use on train journeys. In their car Porterhouse stretched out on the children's laps. In the back seat with Porterhouse on top of them they felt as if they were covered by the thickest fur rug.

'Next year when I replace the car we'll have one with a sunshine roof,' their father promised. 'Then you won't feel nearly so warm.'

At Whitsun a friend had lent them a furnished cottage in the country and Porterhouse fitted into it well. He lay under the apple trees with apple blossom tangled in his shining fur. Bumblebees plundered the dandelions around him, and house martins swooped overhead as they carried mud from the stream for their new nests, but Porterhouse took little notice.

'I must relax while I can,' he declared sleepily. 'Once we are home I shall have little spare time. Your father has been so good naturally I must do all I can to help things along.'

Felicity looked up.

'What things?' she asked.

'In his practice, of course,' said Porterhouse. 'In such a busy house as yours I must do all I can to pull my weight.'

'But Miss Needlepoint does everything that needs doing with the patients,' said Felicity. 'She always has. She doesn't even like it if Mummy offers to post off the boxes of false teeth, and she was really upset one Bob-A-Job-Week when Rory polished the plate outside the front door.'

Porterhouse rolled over on to his back and licked the sun-warmed fur on his chest as if he was counting each hair.

'You see it was because of Miss Needlepoint we never had any animals before,' said Joy, 'and if you upset her she might want to leave.'

'And Daddy would never be able to find another receptionist who was half so good,' added Felicity. 'However much he hated it he might easily decide it was you who ought to go instead.'

Rory scowled at his sister as the big cat looked up.

'Of course Daddy would never decide that,' he said; 'but Miss Needlepoint has made much less fuss about your being here than we expected and you must be careful.'

Porterhouse resumed his wash.

'Up to now our paths have hardly crossed,' he said. 'When they do I'm sure we shall get along with one another pretty well. The small services which I have in mind can't possibly bother her. Miss Needlepoint will mind her business and I shall mind mine.'

'I'm sure whatever Porterhouse is thinking of doing will upset her,' said Felicity gloomily when they were alone; 'but now he's decided to help I don't see what we can do to stop him.'

4 On Duty

Porterhouse began his new duties the day after their return. As soon as Rory and his sisters left for school Porterhouse washed the last traces of porridge and cream from his face and took up his position in the hall, ready to welcome the dentist's first patient. The sun shone on his broad chest and his white whiskers curled like sprung wire. Even Mrs Cooper's electric floor-polisher didn't shift him if it bumped his ample haunches. And however punctually Miss Needlepoint arrived Porterhouse was in the hall before her.

As she donned her white overall and tidied her hair in the office his large golden eyes were always upon her. Now and then he glanced at the grandfather clock or shifted his velvet-smooth paws as if to show that not one of his own hairs was out of place. All the time as she searched for a hair-grip or sharpened a pencil he purred.

'Now then, nice pussy, I think we'll pop you into the garden,' Miss Needlepoint said on the second day she found the big cat in the hall. 'Someone's sure to trip over you.'

Porterhouse only twitched his ear. He never ceased

to purr as she half lifted and half pushed him through the garden door and down the steps. He was back at his post thoughtfully licking one paw before she had answered two calls on the telephone.

'I hope he's not being a bother,' Mrs Cooper asked on her way upstairs to tidy the rooms. 'Usually he's quite happy with me in the kitchen, but lately nothing will keep him there. He seems to want to watch everything that goes on.'

'Of course he's no trouble to me,' said Miss Needlepoint with a laugh. 'I'm really far too busy to notice him.'

But she did, even if it was only out of the corner of her eye, as she escorted a patient into the surgery.

Once the morning's work was under way Porterhouse left the hall for the waiting-room. Leaving the chairs for the patients he stretched out on the table across piles of *Country Life*, the *Geographical Magazine*, and the *Illustrated London News*. The noise of his purr filled the quiet room and the sun gleamed on his tabby fur. Outside the window bees buzzed round the pink geraniums set in the window-box, and the spotted net curtains moved gently in the summer breeze. In the waiting-room Mr Cooper's patients forgot their troubles and whispered to one another about the cat.

'That's never that scrap of a kitten Mr Cooper found in the shelter on the front?'

'It is, you know! Mr Cooper was telling me how the cat had filled out when he was doing my last filling. As proud as Punch he was of him.'

Only Miss Needlepoint frowned at Porterhouse as she bustled in and out.

'I really can't think why he will come in here,' she complained as she straightened the magazines. 'I'll shoo him out.'

For once the patients objected with unusual spirit.

'Why, he's doing no harm. Please let him stay. My little girl's as happy as a sandboy with him to stroke. I've never known a cat with such a way with children.'

Miss Needlepoint was too busy to argue. Porterhouse resettled himself on the magazines and resumed his nap. Even when toddlers stroked his head with sticky fingers he only twitched his ear and went on purring.

Several of the youngest patients refused to accompany Miss Needlepoint into the surgery for their treatment unless the big cat went with them.

'Of course let Porterhouse come too,' said Mr Cooper on the first occasion. 'I'm sure he'll be no trouble.'

And Porterhouse had sat quietly in a corner of the surgery till the work was done. Afterwards, he had escorted the patient to the front door purring loudly and with his ringed tail waving like a flag.

Every week news of the friendly cat at Mr Cooper's spread. More and more children came to have their teeth cared for by Mr Cooper. They came on Saturdays, and after school, on their way to the beach to bathe, with costumes rolled under their arms, or with tennis rackets and cricket bats. Dolls' prams and scooters and brightly painted bicycles crowded the pavement outside, and toffee papers had to be swept up from the porch.

'It's not Mr Cooper they want to see at all but that cat,' Miss Needlepoint complained to her friend at the oculist's as they lunched together. 'The waiting-room is crammed with kiddies. It's just like a school treat, especially on half-holidays. Now they've taken to bringing Porterhouse toys and tit-bits. Catnip mice and even tinned pet-foods are well enough, but more than once I've found herring bones on the very latest copy of *Vogue* and a fish and chip paper poked down behind the window-box. I caught one little girl red-handed as she opened a tin of pilchards in tomato sauce, and another child pouring condensed milk into the saucer under the maidenhair fern.'

'The very idea,' said her friend, with the sun glinting on her upswept, crystal-pink spectacles. 'You told Mr Cooper, of course?'

'Naturally. I considered it no more than my duty.'

'And what did he say?'

Miss Needlepoint frowned as she spooned up the last of her ice cream with fudge and nut sauce. Only worry had made her choose such a sweet pudding, and she would be uneasy until she had brushed her teeth.

'That he hoped Porterhouse had enjoyed the pilchards even though he usually preferred them without tomato sauce,' she said. 'And yesterday, right by that pile of *Reader's Digests* on the waiting-room table, I found a bowl with CAT printed on it that Mr Cooper must have put there himself. He's even provided a tin-opener. Where that cat's concerned he just won't see reason, and the size of it now you wouldn't credit. I told Mr Cooper it wasn't natural for any cat to grow that fast, but he only laughed and said obviously it was natural for Porterhouse and he was a credit to us all.' Miss Needlepoint didn't meet her companion's eye as she rose from the table and prepared to leave. 'You'll hardly believe it, but since that cat came into the house I dread the moment when I have to go back to work. Now everything's changed. It's almost as if he has taken my place.'

Her companion looked up at her with surprise.

'Surely that's rather absurd,' she said. 'You really mustn't magnify your little problem out of all proportion.'

'Porterhouse is out of proportion,' retorted Miss Needlepoint shortly. 'I can assure you it is far from a little problem to one who has to live with it daily.'

'You can tell Miss Needlepoint is annoyed about Porterhouse,' Felicity remarked to the others a few days later. 'She never even smiled when Daddy suggested she typed "Procrastination is the Thief of Teeth" on the top of those reminders he sends to patients who are late coming in for a check up. However helpful Porterhouse means to be we'll have to ask him to stop.'

'But he loves helping,' objected Rory, 'and Daddy likes it too. He told Mummy the medical officer said the school children's teeth had never been so free of dental decay for years, and Porterhouse ought to have half the credit for making them want to come.'

'All the same we'll have to tell him,' insisted Felicity. 'He's bound to understand if we do it properly.'

But Porterhouse didn't. He was concerned and helpful, but somehow, however long they talked, he missed the point.

'I only wish one of you had spoken of this before,' he said gravely with all the tabby lines on his forehead drawn together in a frown. 'Then I would have made a greater effort to share her burden. Obviously the good woman is tired and overwrought and I should have done more.'

Felicity met her sister's eyes and Rory frowned.

'You've done heaps as it is,' he said. 'We only thought with the weather getting warmer you'd rather be outside in the garden.'

'You see Miss Needlepoint likes to work alone,' said Felicity.

'And she's not used to animals,' added Joy. 'When you jump on her lap while she's having her morning coffee it really upsets her. Even when you rub your head against her knee she doesn't see you only mean to be friendly.'

'Now you're so big it's like being charged with a battering ram,' said Felicity.

'One wishes to be polite,' said Porterhouse, 'especially to a fellow worker. However, if you're sure she won't think me uncivil I can easily drop the usual pleasantries.'

For a while after their chat Miss Needlepoint seemed resigned to the big cat's presence in the hall and waiting-room. He was careful not to ladder her stockings or to rub against her nylon overall. Once, when he stood aside as she sped into the surgery, Miss Needlepoint halted to stroke him and the big cat's head pushed against her hand with the force of strongly sprung wire.

'I must say the smaller children are easier to manage when Porterhouse is about,' Miss Needlepoint told her friend from the oculist's as they sat on the pier. 'I'm not one for new-fangled methods but Mr Cooper has certainly set a new trend. I hear that old Mr Toadflax, who practises near the Corn Exchange, has purchased two budgerigars for his waiting-room, and that young dentist out at the new housing estate has tried to go one better by having a vivarium and stick insects in the surgery itself.'

'Porterhouse really has tried not to worry her,' Felicity said to the others. 'He always makes sure children aren't late for their appointments however much they want to go on playing with him, and he never really races her to the front door when the bell rings. Sometimes he stops to wash his back leg half-way along the hall simply so that Miss Needlepoint can welcome the patient first.'

'And once the holidays begin it will be even better because he's bound to want to be with us in the garden,' said Joy. 'I'm sure Porterhouse has only been so interested in Daddy's work because he was bored and there was nothing else for him to do.'

Only Rory was still uneasy. Seated in a corner of the receptionist's office the big cat's ears twitched as Miss Needlepoint took a telephone call or arranged a new appointment for a patient. Once, when having his own teeth stopped, Rory caught sight of Porterhouse erect on a chair at the far end of the surgery with his amber eyes intent on every detail of the treatment. Even Porterhouse's tabby fur smelt of toothpaste and mouth-wash tablets because he often took a nap in the out-house where the empty cartons were kept. And somctimes when they were alone, just by a chance remark Rory would notice how much Porterhouse knew of his father's practice.

'Today that little girl from the dance troop on the pier is coming in again. That regulation plate your father made for her has brought her teeth into line very nicely.'

'That new water-cooled drill of your father's couldn't be bettered. He's delighted with its performance.'

'Young Ken Baker was back again yesterday with three more cavities. Your father told him if he doesn't go easy on sweets he won't have a tooth left in his head by the time he's twenty.'

And something happened soon after which proved that Rory's misgivings were right.

'We're going to spend all the rest of today on the beach,' Felicity told Porterhouse on the first really warm Sunday of the summer when she and the others came in from church. 'Daddy hasn't had a whole day away from the practice for ages. So long as he's here one of the patients always rings up and he says he'll see them even when they haven't really bad toothache at all.'

'It's a shame you can't come too,' said Joy, 'but the sands are sure to be packed, and now you're so large people do stare.'

'But we've put the sardine-sandwich trimmings in with your lights for lunch,' said Rory, 'and we've left you heaps of milk because this weather Mummy says it's bound to go sour.'

Porterhouse rolled over on the swinging seat in the garden. The springs creaked and the fringed canopy moved gently in the summer breeze.

'A break will be good for you all, especially your father,' he told them. 'I shall be quite comfortable holding the fort here. No doubt it will be as well for someone who knows the ropes to be about.'

They were all too busy preparing for their day out to pay much attention to Porterhouse's words. Half an hour later he saw the family off at the front door.

'You'll take good care of everything, won't you, old chap?' said Mr Cooper with a smile as he gave Porterhouse a final caress. The big cat purred in assent.

Once the family had left Porterhouse did not return to his seat in the garden. With the dentist's words still ringing in his ears he made his way down the hall towards the receptionist's office. There, seated upright on the desk with his front paws pricking the blotter, he waited with his eyes on the telephone. Miss Needlepoint's typewriter stood covered and locked, her white overall hung limp on its hook, and for the moment he was in sole command.

The Coopers returned just before supper, glowing with sunburn and laden with damp bathing dresses and sandy sandwich-tins. While the others prepared the meal Rory went to find Porterhouse. Even his sisters did not notice the sound of a heated argument which came from behind the office door. For once Rory sounded really annoyed and upset with the big cat.

'What you've done now is simply crazy! Goodness knows what the telephone exchange must have thought. It's a wonder they didn't send round an engineer. When Daddy asked you to take care of everything of course he never meant that. You ought to have seen how complicated it will be.'

When Rory joined them at supper he still looked excited and flushed. Porterhouse padded round the table, purring loudly as if, in spite of anything which had been said, he was still well pleased with his day's work. In Miss Needlepoint's office a few tabby hairs clung to the blotting paper and the appointment book lay open by the 'phone.

Rory seemed no more cheerful the following morning, even though a large box of chocolates had arrived by post from their grandmother in Ireland. The battered box bore a picture of wild mountain ponies at full gallop. There was a letter inside scented with peppermint creams.

'Granny won the chocolates in a raffle,' their mother explained after she had studied it. 'She's sent them to you to share. She says it's a shame Rory mustn't eat any because chocolates make him so sick, but she thought at least he might like to have the box.'

'We'll put it on your chest-of-drawers,' said Felicity as they ran upstairs with the unexpected gift after breakfast. 'You'll be able to keep heaps of things inside because it's such a huge one.'

'And Felicity and I will write most of the "thank you" letter,' promised Joy. 'You can do just the bit at the end before our names and the kisses.'

But Rory hardly lingered to admire the chocolate-box. He cleaned his teeth and packed his satchel at record speed, and was downstairs ready in the hall a full ten minutes earlier than they usually set off for school.

'Why on earth are you in such a fuss to start?' Felicity called as he urged them to hurry for the second time. 'Joy's only looking for note-paper and an envelope so that we can write most of Gran's letter at school, and we've piles of time.'

'Not if we have to wait ages to cross the road because of the traffic,' urged Rory with his eyes on the front door. 'Besides, we don't want to be here when the first patients arrive. That's always a fuss.'

'Well, it's too late already,' said Felicity as she and her sister scurried down stairs. 'That's the surgery bell now.'

The children stood aside as Miss Needlepoint hurried down the hall with Porterhouse close behind her. The big cat's ears were pricked and every whisker was curled.

'It's Mr Stable, the Vet,' whispered Felicity as the receptionist opened the door and smiled inquiringly at the man who stood on the step with a scarf wrapped round his swollen jaw.

'My appointment was at a quarter to nine, but I've come a bit sooner because this tooth is so painful,' he told the receptionist. 'The sooner it's out the better. I was most relieved that Mr Cooper was able to fit me in. When I 'phoned after lunch yesterday I never really expected anyone would be home to take a message.'

'But no one was,' said Miss Needlepoint as the Vet hurried into the waiting-room with Porterhouse at his side. 'Mr Cooper told me himself that they meant to spend all day on the sands. I offered to come round to take any calls, but he said just for once we wouldn't bother.'

'Well, someone certainly took mine,' said Mr Stable, sitting down carefully in the armchair to which Porterhouse had guided him. 'The voice did seem faint but I thought it must be an elderly neighbour or relation. Directly I explained about this wretched tooth no one could have been more helpful. I was assured that Mr Cooper would see me first thing today and advised not to have any breakfast so that I could have it pulled out with a general anaesthetic. Whoever it was really seemed quite knowledgeable. I remember the exact words – "It's far the best way with a difficult tooth. There will be just a prick in your arm like a scratch from a kitten's claw when it's at play, and then you won't feel another thing." '

Miss Needlepoint frowned as she opened the appointment book and studied the crowded pages. Porterhouse sat with his eyes cast down on his paws.

'I'm sure you'll find the appointment has been properly entered,' said Mr Stable. 'Whoever spoke to me promised faithfully that it would be.'

'It certainly seems in order,' Miss Needlepoint admitted. 'And naturally Mr Cooper will see you just as this says.'

She stared hard at Rory as she led the veterinary surgeon into the surgery. Without waiting for his sisters Rory made for the front door.

'We'll be late too if we don't go after him,' said Joy but Felicity tugged her into the waiting-room where the appointment book still lay open on the table.

'There's the entry that puzzled Miss Needlepoint,' she said. ' "Monday 8.45 emergency appointment for Mr Stable. Possible extrachion." Even though it's written in block letters I'm sure it was Rory who made it. That's how he always spells extraction.'

Joy stared. 'But how could he possibly have taken that call when he was with us all day?'

'Rory may have been,' said Felicity, 'but Porterhouse wasn't. He took that call and gave Rory the message.'

5 The Only Way

'Naturally I did what I could even if it meant leaving the receiver to dangle till Rory came home,' Porterhouse admitted when the twins confronted him in the garden after tea. 'Mr Stable has always been most kind. When I had that nasty upset after those herrings and the Cornish cream he was round with a remedy within the hour. On Sunday when I was able to nudge off the receiver with my paw and take his call I could hardly ignore his own appeal for help. And I'm happy to say his tooth came out this morning without a hitch. Your father told him that he'll be back on his rounds and right as rain by tomorrow.'

'Well, none of us will be,' said Felicity gloomily. 'Daddy's gone to a dental conference in Bristol today, but when he comes back tomorrow he wants Rory to give him a full explanation.'

'It was Miss Needlepoint who made most fuss,' explained Joy. 'She insisted on Daddy finding out who gave Rory that message and now he'll have to.'

Porterhouse stopped purring as he noticed their troubled faces. He nudged Felicity's knee so that his ear turned inside out. The fur of his cheek was thick and sun-warmed against her bare leg. Since his afternoon in charge of the dentist's practice Porterhouse had changed. He looked older and twice as large. The ball he had played with as a kitten lay chewed and forgotten in a corner of the tool shed.

'Possibly if you think it would help I might have a word with your father on his return myself,' Porterhouse suggested.

'Of course it wouldn't,' said Felicity shortly. 'You'll have to leave it to Rory now.'

'No doubt that will be best,' agreed Porterhouse comfortably. 'He's never short of ideas, and I'm sure by tomorrow he'll come up with something.'

'I can't see what,' said Joy. 'He thought so hard today at school that he was bottom in nearly everything, besides dropping two catches at cricket. Now he's gone straight upstairs to his room and bolted the door so that he can think by himself till bed time.'

Mr Cooper frowned as he cycled home from the station next day. He was as mystified by what had occurred as his receptionist. Once Rory had made up his mind not to share a secret, making him do so was like prising a limpet off a rock at low tide. Yet Miss Needlepoint would never be satisfied until he discovered who had taken the 'phone call and passed on the details to his son.

His receptionist had discussed the puzzle in hushed tones throughout the remainder of the morning whenever she handed him an amalgam filling or replaced the glass of mouth-wash by the dental chair. Miss Needlepoint liked everything to be neat and reasonable. What had occurred was neither. Like someone finding themselves on shifting quicksand she had struggled to discover a reasonable explanation.

'Are you sure you hadn't asked a neighbour to drop in and take any calls?' she had suggested to Mr Cooper as they waited for a patient's filling to harden. 'Do you think that paper-boy may have heard the 'phone ringing and climbed in through that window you left ajar for the cat?'

'The newspaper came just before we left,' Mr Cooper had explained, 'and the milkman was even earlier.'

Even when Mr Cooper was astride his bicycle outside the house ready to leave for the station, Miss Needlepoint had run down the steps after him.

'Of course it might have been a burglar who answered the 'phone simply to stop it ringing. Even the most hardened criminal might have felt sorry for someone with such nasty toothache, and perhaps he jotted down the details that Rory found.'

'Then Rory would most certainly have told us,' Mr Cooper had told her with a smile. 'Anything like a burglar breaking in he would never have been able to keep under his hat. Now you're not to give the matter another thought. There's obviously some perfectly simple explanation, and once I've seen Rory we'll know all about it.'

Weaving his way through the heavy holiday traffic Mr Cooper felt hot and cross. Talking to Rory before bed time meant giving up a bathe before supper. Whatever Rory had to say, Mr Cooper was determined to make it plain that in future he mustn't interfere with the practice or do anything to upset Miss Needlepoint.

As Mr Cooper dismounted outside his house he paused and looked up with a frown. In the play-room the record-player and radio were silent and the curtains of his son's bedroom were drawn against the light.

'I'm afraid Rory has had a wretched tummy upset,' his wife told him as he hurried indoors. 'The doctor says it's nothing serious but he's feeling pretty seedy and I've kept him in bed. He's half asleep now so I shouldn't go up.'

Upstairs Rory lay still in the darkened bedroom. He tried hard not to remember what he had eaten. Instead, he thought about the touching final scene at his death bed, and tombstones. After he had gone perhaps his family would leave his room just as it was now with his Churchill stamps soaking in a saucer on the window sill, a long-division sum unfinished in the exercise book in his satchel, the dried piece of bubble gum still stuck to the bottom of the waste-paper basket, and the chocolate box on the chest-of-drawers.

Thinking of the chocolates Rory stiffened. Only picturing his tombstone stopped him from being sick again. He thought he would have a tombstone of shiny brown marble with green chips in the kerb that would save weeding and shine as bright as chopped up jelly. An urn with angels would be nice on top, and a marble book bearing a simple inscription across its pages. As Rory lay composing the words he fell asleep.

He hardly stirred two hours later when his sisters

looked in to say 'good night'. Porterhouse followed at their heels treading softly.

Their brother's face was only a white blur in the darkness. Only a nightlight glimmered on the chest-of-drawers, casting shadows over the ponies which galloped across the lid of the chocolate box.

At the sound of Porterhouse's purring Rory opened his eyes and ran his finger through the cat's thick fur.

'We're sorry you've been so sick,' said Felicity; 'but at least it's stopped Daddy asking questions. Mummy said he wasn't to worry you on any account.'

'And tomorrow he'll be busy with two impacted wisdom teeth and a full upper and lower plate so he's bound to forget all about it,' said Joy. 'Even Miss Needlepoint's only worried now to know how you are and what made you so sick.'

'And what on earth did?' asked Felicity.

As she spoke her sister reached for the chocolate box and lifted the lid. Only pleated paper cups fluttered to the floor as she felt for a sweet.

'There's not a single chocolate left, and the box was almost full,' she said staring at Felicity. 'Who can have eaten them?'

'I did,' said Rory. 'Even the chocolates with green marzipan centres and those with strawberry syrup under the pink cream. After the top row I felt so awful I nearly stopped; then I remembered how beastly it would be if everyone knew about Porterhouse being so different from other cats, and I went on and finished the lot. I knew exactly what would happen if I did, but it seemed the only way.'

6 Food For Thought

'Now that you've broken up for the holidays do try and keep Porterhouse out of Miss Needlepoint's way,' their mother told Rory and the twins a few days later. 'Yesterday on her way to answer the 'phone she tripped over him in the hall and it could have been a really nasty tumble.'

'I was coming downstairs when that happened,' Felicity told the others when they were alone. 'Miss Needlepoint was in such a hurry Porterhouse hadn't a chance to jump out of the way. It was only a mercy Mummy was too fussed to notice what Miss Needlepoint said when she helped her up.'

'Why?' asked Joy. 'What did she say?'

'That it was entirely her fault for not looking where she was going,' said Felicity, 'but she had wanted to reach the telephone *before anyone else took the call.* She was looking straight at Porterhouse when she said that and I'm sure she's suspicious.'

'Then why didn't she make Daddy ask Rory to explain properly about that telephone call from Mr Stable directly he was well enough to answer questions?' asked her sister.

'Because of what she was afraid Daddy might find

out,' explained Felicity. 'Deep down Miss Needlepoint's scared Porterhouse must have had something to do with it, and she doesn't want to be certain.'

Rory frowned as he looked at their solemn faces.

'Of course she doesn't suspect anything,' he said firmly, 'and if Porterhouse chooses to be in the waiting-room most of the time I don't see why we should stop him. Everyone's just fussing. When he's asleep on the table with the magazines no one could fall over him again, and he can't possibly do any harm.'

Only the next morning Rory was to realize just how mistaken he had been.

For the first time in all the years she had worked there Miss Needlepoint arrived at the dentist's house well over ten minutes late. As she sped up the steps she found the front door ajar, while from the waiting-room came the sound of cheerful voices mingled with Porterhouse's most contented purr.

When Miss Needlepoint strode into the waiting-room she saw Porterhouse stretched across the magazines on the table while the patients sat round him in a smiling semi-circle. A mother with two young children, and with a toddler on her lap, sat on the cat's right hand. To his left, in the most comfortable armchair, a shop girl from the town sat with a handkerchief pressed to her swollen jaw. Nearest the door was a traveller with toothpaste samples.

'Don't you hurry yourself,' said the mother kindly as Miss Needlepoint fastened the last button of her overall. 'No one was about when we arrived but the door was open and the nice pussy showed us in. He was waiting on the step cheerful as you please just as though he was looking out for the lot of us. Mr Cooper has an emergency in with him now and this young lady with toothache is to follow. My kiddics were booked for the first appointment but with pussy to play with we won't mind waiting one little bit.'

From the table Porterhouse met Miss Needlepoint's glance without a blink. His purr never stopped. It filled the sunny room like the hum of bumblebees at noon-day.

For the rest of the morning Miss Needlepoint carried out her duties with her usual calm and meticulous care. She recorded appointments neatly in the book, her hand never trembled as she assisted Mr Cooper in the surgery, and her smile was professionally reassuring as she settled each patient in the dental chair.

Rory, who had witnessed most of what had happened and been just too late to interfere, was puzzled but pleased by her behaviour.

But the others were doubtful. The calm of their father's receptionist seemed much more like the uncanny stillness before a storm.

At lunch time when the last patient had gone, with a set face Miss Needlepoint hurried into the kitchen and closed the door. Even from the garden Rory and his sisters could not fail to hear what Miss Needlepoint said to their mother. The words that she had held in check throughout the morning tumbled out with the force of a mountain stream in full spate.

'That cat knew what he was doing. This morning he deliberately took advantage. For months now I've sensed him waiting for his chance and today when my alarm failed he took it. He pounced like a cat on a mouse! If you'd only seen him sitting in my waiting-room pleased as Punch, and with such a look in his eye, you'd know I wasn't exaggerating. In all my life I would never have credited such interference. The front door may have been on the latch. With kiddies running in and out one must make allowances, but as sure as I'm standing here, that cat must have been waiting on the front step simply to take over my job and show the patients inside.'

The children did not wait to hear any more. They retreated to the foot of the garden. Soon after they heard their mother back the car out of the garage and they guessed she had decided to take Miss Needlepoint home.

'You'll have to talk to Porterhouse,' Felicity told Rory after they had helped their father dish up a very late lunch. 'Daddy can't understand why Miss Needlepoint was so upset. He thinks she's over-tired and imagining things, but even he says Porterhouse had better be kept out of her way if he gets on her nerves.'

'And it's Porterhouse's fault,' said Joy. 'He must have known Miss Needlepoint minds being late for anything. He did it just to upset her. He's been waiting for weeks and it was just awful of him. After arranging that appointment for Mr Stable he imagines he can get away with anything.'

'And if you don't stop him now you'll never be able to,' added her sister.

Rory went in search of Porterhouse directly after their meal. From the bathroom window Felicity and Joy watched him trail down the garden.

'He'll do it better if we leave him alone,' said Felicity. 'Once Rory's decided he'll know what to say.'

At the foot of the garden Porterhouse sat up very straight. The tips of his ears nearly reached the yellow circles of the sunflowers which grew against the boundary fence. Rory faced the large cat with his hands clasped behind his back.

'It was taking advantage and not fair,' he told Porterhouse. 'You did it on purpose just to annoy her. Even if Daddy was pleased not to be kept waiting you're never to interfere with the patients or Miss Needlepoint again. She'll leave if you do. And if Daddy had to choose between her and you he might easily decide to keep Miss Needlepoint.'

Porterhouse looked down at his paws. For a moment his purr was silenced. The garden with its worn strip of grass and untidy August flower beds was shadowed. Slowly Porterhouse looked up into Rory's troubled face.

'It will be a wrench, of course,' he said. 'The work has been of great interest, but now that you have made the position plain and since you think it wise, naturally I shall withdraw my services and leave Miss Needlepoint to manage on her own.'

And as the sun blazed out from behind a cloud and Rory rubbed the cat's deep fur he purred again.

Rory said little when he joined his sisters. They guessed he had minded saying what had needed to be said.

'Of course Porterhouse understood,' he told Felicity when she asked. 'He's promised not to upset Miss Needlepoint again. He never meant her to be really upset. It was just a game. Once I explained he said he'd stop directly. Only he really did enjoy helping with the patients, and now he's giving it up we'll have to find him another really good outside interest to make up for it.'

Fortunately what Porterhouse needed proved to be far nearer than they guessed.

Now that the school holidays had begun Mrs Clarence's guest-house next door was always crowded. Porterhouse dropped in regularly for tit-bits.

'The girl in the kitchen is most cordial,' he reported. 'Hardly a day goes by without some small offering: boiled milk left over from the breakfast coffee, a burnt rice pudding or the remains of a fish pie.'

'But you can't possibly be all that hungry,' objected Felicity.

'Even if a call is merely social it wouldn't do to refuse,' Porterhouse explained. 'I try to oblige even with the custard left over from prunes.'

The sun shone on his striped fur as he shouldered his way along the guest-house garden wall, past the Morello cherry and the star-fish blossoms of the striped mauve clematis. Soon he was as familiar with the guest-house garden as he was with their own.

At lunch Porterhouse lay on the veranda outside the dining-room watching every bowl of Windsor soup or slice of luncheon meat which the guests ate.

Soon all the guests knew him. Porterhouse was on the lawn to greet them as they walked hungrily to and fro before breakfast at nine-thirty; and he was there at night, when damp bathing dresses hung from the bed-room windows, and the guests watched television in the lounge.

Once a departing guest wrote of him affectionately in the visitors' book. He was also clearly featured in a photograph of the guest-house on the cover of Mrs Clarence's new brochure.

Every time Mrs Clarence looked at the photograph and saw Porterhouse on the front steps, with his tabby stripes looped round his ample chest like a mayor's chain of office, she frowned.

'No one can say I'm not a lover of all dumb creatures,' Mrs Clarence explained to Mr Cooper as he attended to a troublesome back molar, 'but a cat of Porterhouse's build does do damage. My guests are always welcome to bring along their dogs and there have been complaints. One little poodle had to be taken home after only a week with us. She was just a bundle of nerves, and a corgi who came this week-end is almost as bad.'

Mrs Clarence only stopped talking when Mr Cooper was ready to fill her cavity with amalgam and put four cotton wool rolls into her mouth, with a metal mould and a hooked siphon to suck up the drips.

‘Porterhouse never chases the dogs at the guesthouse,’ Rory told his father when he passed on the complaint. ‘They try to chase him. Only when he just stands and looks at them the dogs don’t understand.’

‘And it wasn’t Porterhouse who broke her garden frame,’ said Joy, ‘but a boxer puppy who saw him rather suddenly in the moonlight and bolted round the garden howling.’

‘Porterhouse wasn’t all that bigger than him either,’ added Rory. ‘It’s just that he seems larger in the dark like that dog with eyes as big as tea cups in the Tinder Box story.’

It was a relief to them all when Porterhouse forgot about the dogs and spent most of the time in the hotel summerhouse with one of the older residents. She was an elderly lady always clad in a faded coat and skirt, a white straw hat, and white canvas shoes. She was never parted from a brown and fawn leather carrier bag which bulged with papers.

‘She writes all the time,’ said Felicity, ‘and she can’t just be answering letters because no one would have so many. Porterhouse just sits and watches. He never leaves except when she goes up to her room. It’s on the top floor just the same as our back box-room. When the light’s on at night you can see inside from the bottom of the garden.’

Porterhouse was unusually vague about his new friend when they questioned him.

‘That’s Miss Wellcome. She has her room at reduced rates in the winter months. Unfortunately now the guest-house is full for the summer the charge will go up and she'll have to make a change.'

'But where will Miss Wellcome go?' asked Felicity. 'Mummy tried to find a room for someone this week and there was nothing vacant in the whole town except in those really expensive hotels on the front.'

Porterhouse didn't reply. He sat with the tabby marks wrinkled on his brow as if he was lost in thought.

The weather was warm and they spent most of their time on the beach. None of them noticed that the old lady no longer shared the summerhouse with Porterhouse till several days later.

'Miss Wellcome must have found somewhere else to live,' Felicity reported one night when she ran in from the garden. 'There are bunk beds in her room now and two girls with a transistor radio.'

During the following days Porterhouse was unusually quiet. Once Rory found him in the spare room inspecting the divan.

'I was only looking to see if the room might be suitable,' the big cat said.

'For what?' asked Rory.

'Letting, of course,' said Porterhouse. 'If it's a spare room your parents can't need it.'

'Well, they do,' said Rory. 'Gran sleeps there whenever she comes over from Ireland.'

'What did Porterhouse say then?' Felicity asked when Rory told his sisters what had occurred.

'That he would have to think of something else,'

reported Rory, 'but he looked quite disappointed and worried.'

Porterhouse was seated in a corner of the dining-room that day at lunch when his father advised Rory to have a second helping of fish.

'You know what Bertie Wooster always says about Jeeves and his sardines,' he told him with a smile. 'There's nothing like fish for the brain.'

No one paid much attention to the remark but from that moment Porterhouse refused all other foods except fish.

'He never used to be so fussy,' complained Mrs Cooper after cooking a conger eel from the fish market. 'Now the weather's so warm he'll have to make do with tinned meat.'

Porterhouse was in the garden licking an empty pot of fishpaste when they told him of their mother's decision.

'Even Daddy thinks you need a more balanced diet,' said Felicity; 'and we could smell your cods' heads being boiled all over the house.'

'Of course your mother mustn't put herself out on my account,' Porterhouse told them. 'In future I must try to make my own arrangements.'

He gazed thoughtfully into the goldfish pool and dabbled his paw in the water.

The girls shivered as the big cat stalked away.

'Of course Porterhouse didn't mean he would eat our goldfish,' said Rory but in his heart he wasn't so sure. He was glad there were no other fish in the town much nearer than the lake in the municipal park.

It was Rory who first saw the policeman the next day from the attic window while they were looking out rummage for the church bazaar. At first the policeman only looked like a blot of blue-black ink as he pushed his bicycle slowly up the hill towards their Crescent.

The policeman mounted his cycle near the crest of the hill. For several minutes Rory lost sight of him till he rounded the corner of the Crescent.

'A policeman's cycling up our street,' Rory told his sister. 'He's the one Daddy had to see so often about his false teeth because he had such a difficult bite.'

'Well, he's not coming here today,' said Felicity as she joined Rory at the window. 'He's gone to the guest-house next door.'

The sight of the constable's bicycle propped against the kerb and the policeman in conversation with Mrs Clarence at the door interested them all.

'Perhaps he's looking for an escaped criminal,' suggested Joy. 'Probably there will be a siege and we'll be able to help.'

Beside her Rory looked less cheerful as he leant far out of the window and strained his ears to catch what Mrs Clarence was saying. Her voice was indignant as she addressed the constable.

'With a creature that size I knew something of this sort would happen in time. It's not that I haven't spoken before as nicely as possible but it's had no effect. He's over my wall and into the garden at all hours of the day.

Liberty hall you might call it. Naturally one doesn't wish to cause unpleasantness, especially with a neighbour, but I really think this time the matter must be cleared up.'

Even as the policeman emerged from the guest-house porch and stood on the pavement mopping his brow, they knew he was about to mount their own steps and ring the door bell.

'I'm sure it's about Porterhouse,' said Rory as he met his sisters' eyes. 'We'd better go down. We can't leave Mummy to see him alone.'

In the kitchen the policeman stood with a notebook in his hand. Even the sight of his false teeth which reflected so much of their father's skill didn't do much to make them feel less uncomfortable.

'I'm afraid Mrs Clarence next door has had a serious loss,' their mother explained. 'It will cause her a lot of trouble especially at such a busy time. A whole fresh salmon which the fishmonger had just delivered for lunch has disappeared from her kitchen.'

'As clean as a whistle from the table while the maid popped upstairs,' said the policeman. 'Fins, tail and all.'

'So the constable came here to see if we had heard or seen anything suspicious,' said their mother.

The policeman shifted his feet and ran his tongue across his front teeth. They guessed he remembered their father's good work.

'There was some talk of a cat,' he said. 'While not wishing to cast suspicion, Mrs Clarence did wonder if

yours might have been responsible, but I told her no ordinary cat would carry off anything that large.'

Rory swallowed. His eyes were fixed on the garden. Porterhouse lay asleep on the swinging seat, one paw trailed over the side. Below on the grass lay a piece of crumpled greaseproof wrapping and what looked like a fishmonger's bill.

'Our cat isn't exactly an ordinary one,' he said. 'He's extra large and just lately Porterhouse hasn't fancied anything to eat except fish.'

7 No Fixed Abode

'Mistakes will happen,' said Porterhouse firmly when the children reproached him later. 'The kitchen-maid next door has always been most thoughtful. Naturally when I saw that salmon set down on the table by the back door where she usually puts left-overs intended for me, I took it to be another small token and accepted it without a second thought.'

'You should have known without needing a second thought,' retorted Felicity. 'Mrs Clarence always gives her guests something special for lunch on Saturday when they first come. Now they'll have to have corned beef. There isn't another salmon in the whole town. Mummy's rung up three fishmongers to ask.'

'And a salmon like that wasn't a small token,' said Joy. 'Daddy will have to pay £6 os 8d just for your lunch.'

'And supper as well,' corrected Porterhouse, rolling over on the seat so that the springs sagged under his weight; 'with wholemeal breadcrumbs I'm sure there will be more than enough. While the weather is so warm just a snack at bed time is really quite sufficient.'

Porterhouse rocked the seat gently and licked a silver scale from his paw.

'You might mind a bit,' said Felicity. 'Mrs Clarence isn't going to prosecute us but she was really cross.'

'Mummy came to apologize with us,' said Joy, 'and even after she gave her Daddy's cheque Mrs Clarence still didn't cheer up. She thinks some tourists who just stop overnight will never come again. In her brochure it says "high class cuisine" and no one could call corned beef that. There wasn't even an exciting pudding to make up – just rice flavoured with chocolate, or biscuits and cheese.'

Porterhouse yawned so that the black ridges on the roof of his mouth showed like ridges of sea-washed sand far down his throat.

'I'm sure that, though tiresome, such a trifling setback need cause Mrs Clarence no alarm,' he said sleepily.

The girls left Porterhouse at last. Only Rory lingered. He was still puzzled by the cat's behaviour.

'What I don't see is why you want to eat so much fish anyway,' he said. 'It's not simply that salmon. Lately you've taken kipper heads from the dustbin, and finished up all the crusts when we've had fishpaste sandwiches.'

Porterhouse flexed his front paw round Rory's fist. Before he replied he glanced round to make sure they were alone.

'It's simply that at the moment I need something to help me think,' Porterhouse said. 'Others might manage without anything special but I find it hard. Your father said nothing was better for the brain than a diet of fish, and with his medical training I felt sure he would know.'

'Of course he does,' said Rory, 'but what is it you need to think about so hard? If anything's worrying you we'll all try and help.'

'I'm sure you would,' said Porterhouse giving Rory's dusty knee a rough lick with his burred tongue. 'If the trouble was mine I would have asked you at once. Unfortunately it's not. The friend concerned would never wish to share the trouble with others. I only heard of it myself because even the most shy and proud will sometimes talk most freely to a household cat.'

Rory couldn't sleep that night. He was worried about Porterhouse. Already the cat's determination to help his unknown friend had led him into trouble, and next time it might be even worse. That winter afternoon in the firelit sitting-room when he had wished for a giant pet seemed far away, like a tiny picture viewed through the wrong end of a pair of field-glasses. Now in less than a month Porterhouse would be fully grown and the future seemed full of problems.

Rory twisted and turned. As a clock in the town chimed eleven he jumped out of bed and crept downstairs in search of a glass of water.

'There's someone in the waiting-room with Porterhouse,' Rory whispered as he stood barefoot in the doorway of his sisters' room a few minutes later. 'I've been down for a drink and as I passed I saw the light under the door. Porterhouse was purring just the way he does when one of us rubs his ear.'

The twins sat up and stared.

'Probably one of us forgot to switch off the light,'

said Felicity, 'and Porterhouse has gone in there because it's cool.'

'And he does sometimes purr quite loudly when he's alone,' said Joy. 'If he's really comfortable he forgets to stop.'

'But someone coughed,' said Rory, 'the way people do when they're just waiting.'

Felicity and Joy were suddenly wide awake in the moonlit room.

'Then we ought to tell Daddy,' said Felicity. 'It might be burglars!'

'We can't,' whispered Rory. 'He's written a message on the hall pad for Mummy. The hospital needed him urgently in Casualty. He meant her to see it when she came in from her lecture.'

'Then we'd better tell her,' suggested Joy. 'She should have been back ages ago.'

'But she isn't,' said Rory. 'I've looked. Probably the car's broken down or she's just stopped to talk. She wouldn't worry because she'd think Daddy was sure to be here, but till one of them comes back we're alone in the house.'

They stared at one another. The night was silent. The street was empty. Not even a transistor radio sounded from the guest-house next door. In the distance they could just make out the sound of the waves breaking on the shore.

'We'd better go down,' said Felicity. 'Anything's better than waiting up here.'

The house still felt hot after the heat of the day.

Even the water in Porterhouse's bowl was lukewarm when Rory tripped over it as they tiptoed along the hall. Miss Needlepoint's overall glimmered white on its coat-hanger in her office close by the telephone.

'Shouldn't we dial 999 right away?' Joy suggested as they stood outside the waiting-room door, but the others only signalled to her to listen.

From inside the room came the regular sound of Porterhouse purring and the rustle of pages slowly turned. Now and then the sofa springs creaked as someone rose, crossed to the table, shuffled through the piled magazines, and then sat down again.

'That sounds just like an ordinary patient looking at the magazines while they wait to see Daddy,' whispered Joy.

'Perhaps the waiting-room's haunted by the ghost of a patient who waited there with dreadful toothache ages and ages ago,' suggested Rory.

'Well, if it is only a ghost we needn't fuss,' said Felicity and swung open the door.

Porterhouse lay in his usual place on the table stretched out across piled copies of *Punch*, the *Ladies' Home Journal*, *Country Life*, and *Vogue*. And smiling at them from the sofa was the elderly lady whom they had so often seen with Porterhouse writing in the summerhouse of the guest-house next door.

'I realize I am a trifle early for my appointment at half past nine tomorrow morning,' said Miss Wellcome, 'but I knew dear Mr Cooper wouldn't mind if I dropped in to glance at his magazines and have a short rest.

They are always so very interesting and in this weather one does grow a trifle fatigued.'

Miss Wellcome sat up very straight on the sofa. A pair of grey fabric gloves was folded on her knee and her shoes had been carefully whitened. A sunshade with an ivory handle lay at her side. In a basket at her feet was a carriage clock in a worn leather case, a silver backed hairbrush, a pair of curling tongs, an ivory card case, several brownish photographs in silver frames, and a hot-water bottle. Beside her on the sofa lay the suede shopping bag full of papers which they had seen so often before. At the far end of the room the french window which opened on to a path at the side of the house was ajar.

'Of course Daddy wouldn't mind you waiting,' said Felicity as she latched the window and looked hard at Porterhouse who sat studying his paws. 'Lots of patients do come early if their appointments don't fit in with the buses or it's pouring with rain. But you'll have ages to wait. Wouldn't it be better to go home and come again in the morning?'

Miss Wellcome looked up from her magazine which was open at a double page picture of a summer evening picnic, with a glazed turkey, a boar's head, tall frosted glasses, and a gilt basket of hothouse fruit set on a marble table beside a moonlit swimming pool.

'No doubt that would be wise. Unfortunately at present it's impossible. You see I have no home to go to.'

The children stared. The only sound for a moment was their cat's regular purr.

'We never guessed,' said Felicity. 'When we didn't see you writing in the summerhouse any more we thought you must have gone to another hotel.'

'Though with the town so full we thought it wouldn't have been a bit easy,' added Joy.

'And you were perfectly right,' said Miss Wellcome. 'I have been quite unable to find anywhere suitable at terms which I could afford.'

'But surely you don't live just out-of-doors?' asked Rory before the others could stop him.

'For the moment that is just what I have to do,' said Miss Wellcome simply. 'No doubt when the season ends it will be easier and I shall be settled somewhere before the winter. While I was so comfortably installed next door I wasn't idle and I fancy my work may one day bear fruit. I have good expectations.' As she spoke she glanced at the worn suede shopping bag full of papers on the sofa beside her, and her cheeks flushed red as Beauty of Bath apples.

'But however have you managed?' Felicity asked before Rory could ask their visitor for any more details.

'I was worried at first, I must admit,' said Miss Wellcome. 'When I and my sisters were girls at the rectory our life was perhaps more sheltered than most. We did not even go to camp as young people would today, but I have been most agreeably surprised at what can be done. I hire a deckchair at a most reasonable sum and the beach shelters at night are not too uncomfortable. With no rent to pay I am able to take most of my meals at cafés where I am known, and my washing is done at the launderette in the High Street. The post office is most handy for writing, with ink and blotting paper both provided and more often than not ball-point pens as well.'

'But what about not having a letter-box of your own or a dustbin?' asked Rory.

'And anywhere to wash or heat a kettle?' added Joy.

'And without a single cupboard or chest-of-drawers where do you keep all your things?' asked Felicity.

Miss Wellcome smiled.

'It's simply a matter of adjustment. Instead of a bed-sitting-room the whole town is my home now. I collect my mail from the post office and my rubbish goes into any of the litter bins. There's a nicely kept little cloak-room in a corner of the Park where I go for a wash and brush up, and all my possessions are left in the luggage office at the railway station or the bus depot. You might say that the railway station's luggage office serves as my wardrobe, where I store my overcoats and warmer winter woollies, and the bus station serves as a chest-of-drawers, where I keep anything I may need from day to day in two suitcases and a holdall. Heating a kettle has been one of my greatest difficulties. After several rather nasty little accidents with a picnic stove I've decided to abandon the attempt, but I must admit I've missed the comfort of a really warm hot-water bottle. If the nights turn chilly I often drop into a café for a pot of tea simply to fill my bottle from the hot-water jug.'

'Well, we could fill it for you tonight at least,' said

Felicity quickly. 'The water's always nearly boiling in the heater over the kitchen sink.'

Porterhouse faced them in the kitchen as they filled the bottle.

'It's good of you to take this as you have,' he said as he paused to accept a bowl of milk which Rory had put out for him. 'Naturally I never doubted your hospitality, but taken as it were on the hop I fancied you might have felt I should have asked you first.'

'Of course you should,' said Felicity. 'Then we might have been able to think of something much more sensible.'

Porterhouse washed his face after the milk.

'Unfortunately I was not able to tell even Rory of Miss Wellcome's troubles,' he said. 'I knew she was the last person to wish them to be known. I had to manage alone and this was the best I could think of for the moment. Given the hang of it the window latch is quite easy to open.'

'But how did you explain to Miss Wellcome?' asked Felicity as Rory left with the filled hot-water bottle.

'When I found her tonight in the shelter she was good enough to bring me home,' said Porterhouse. 'I simply led her round by the side path to the french window. Once inside she settled just as I had hoped when I remembered her appointment tomorrow morning.'

As he spoke they heard a car coming up the hill towards their house. Felicity stared at her sister.

'That's Mummy now. When she finds Miss Wellcome what will she say?'

'She won't,' said Rory as he rejoined them. 'I've switched off the waiting-room light and left Miss Wellcome almost asleep. She told me we weren't to give her another thought. She doesn't really care for an early cup of tea. She'll just pop out for an early breakfast before anyone's about and come back for her appointment at half past nine.'

8 Contents of a Shopping Basket

Felicity and Joy were worried and cross the next morning. Rory knew by the noises that came from their room. Drawers were jerked open and shut, doors banged and a sandal shot across the floor. Felicity brushed her hair as if every tangle was an enemy. Rory guessed that both the twins regretted their decision to keep secret Miss Wellcome's presence in the house during the night. As Rory smelt bacon frying and the whole well-ordered machinery of a new working day in the house began he worried too. Still half dressed he scurried downstairs and opened the waiting-room door.

'It's all right, Miss Wellcome's gone now,' Rory told the twins ten minutes later when he found them in the bathroom. 'Porterhouse says she had an excellent night. She's left the room so tidy you would never know anyone had been there, except that she's finished a really difficult *Daily Telegraph* cross-word. She's done a tinned cat food competition too in one of the magazines. The first prize is a holiday châlet or a fully furnished bungalow with oil-fired central heating and enough cat food for a year. It's that brand Porterhouse likes, so I had a label to enclose with her entry and I've posted it already in the box on the corner. Porterhouse says Miss

Wellcome thought for ages about the caption they wanted for their cat food, so it's bound to be better than dozens of the others.'

'Never mind about the competition,' said Felicity. 'Did anyone find out she slept here all night? Joy and I have hardly slept a wink. Daddy or Mummy might easily have gone into the waiting-room any time.'

'Well, they haven't,' retorted Rory, 'and even if they had found her there it wouldn't have been so awful. Porterhouse says he's sure Daddy would understand. What's the point in having a waiting-room if patients can't wait as long as they like in it?'

Felicity turned to face her brother. When she spoke her words were kind but serious.

'We can't always do just as Porterhouse says. He's the largest and kindest animal we've ever known but he's still a cat, and he doesn't understand how difficult it's going to be to help Miss Wellcome. What's happened to her isn't something Porterhouse would be able to put right and we won't be able to do it either, just by wishing. It needs a grown-up who knows all the places where she ought to go to ask for proper help.'

'But Miss Wellcome doesn't want people to know,' said Rory. 'She's never asked anyone for anything all her life. Even at school Porterhouse says she and her sisters weren't allowed to ask for more jam or butter at meals. They had to wait till someone noticed and it was passed.'

'Well, we've noticed,' said Felicity. 'We know what she needs and today when she comes for her appointment we'll have to ask her if we can tell Mummy about it. Once she says "yes" Mummy's sure to know what's best to do.'

'At least we can try,' urged Joy. 'She may pretend it's not so bad to live out-of-doors but it must be terrible for her.'

Unfortunately their plan was upset by their father's receptionist who greeted Miss Wellcome on the doorstep and whisked her into the surgery before they could speak to her.

'We can see her just as easily afterwards,' said Felicity as they retreated upstairs. 'Let's go and make the beds.'

But half an hour later when they returned to the hall, it was a little girl who emerged from the surgery, with two toothpaste samples clutched in her hand and a new sixpence.

'Miss Wellcome, why she left a quarter of an hour ago,' Miss Needlepoint told them. 'Your father only needed to see her for a few minutes. Then I took her straight through the surgery into the workroom. The mechanic needed to check the shade of enamel for her new dental plate, and he promised to show her out by the back way.'

That night they left an extra rug in the waiting-room with a thermos flask full of hot water and some malted milk. Porterhouse promised to unlatch the window.

'But I doubt if she'll come here again,' he said. 'Without an appointment the following day she would not think it right.'

Miss Wellcome did not come again. She seemed to

have been swallowed up by the crowd in the busy seaside town. The children trailed round the streets in search of her. At meal times they peered into the dining-room windows of the cheaper boarding-houses, and checked every caravan in the large caravan site on the outskirts of the town, but there was no sign of her. At night Porterhouse padded along the front under the coloured lights looking in every shelter. They inquired at the public library, and left a letter addressed to Miss Wellcome in the general post office, but the librarian told them Miss Wellcome had not been in for several days, and their letter was never collected.

The weather changed towards the middle of August. Raindrops pitted the surface of the deserted bathing pool, and puddles gathered in the looped canvas of the deck-chairs. Holiday-makers took refuge in the shops, spending their money on giant sticks of rock, yard-long matchboxes, views of the town painted on slices of varnished wood, netted glass floats which would never know the wash of the waves, and sea urchin shells. The fathers wore thick winter socks with their beach sandals, and the bright plastic raincoats of the mothers looked like wrinkled balloons the morning after a dance.

'It's freezing cold and beastly damp,' said Felicity as they huddled round the sitting-room fire. 'Daddy says it's almost as icy on the front as it was in January when he found Porterhouse.'

On the hearth rug the big cat's purr was silent. Listening to the rain they thought of Miss Wellcome who had also found no better refuge than a shelter on the front.

'I expect she went somewhere else to live ages ago,' said Joy. 'Probably relations have taken her in.'

'She told Porterhouse she hadn't any,' said Rory; 'not even a cousin twice removed.'

'Then perhaps she's taken a room in another town which wasn't so full,' suggested Felicity.

'If she had she would have given the post office her new address,' said Rory; 'and she hadn't up to this morning because I asked again.'

The following day the mystery was solved. Rory raced into the play-room after tea. His tears splashed on to Porterhouse's head as the cat hurried forward to comfort him.

'It's Miss Wellcome,' he said. 'I know where she is. Today Miss Needlepoint gave me the false teeth packets to post – just this once because she's taking pottery lessons with her friend from the oculist's and they wanted to have supper first. The top parcel of all was for Miss Wellcome, and why we've none of us seen her again is because she's in hospital with pneumonia. Miss Needlepoint says they found her in one of the beach shelters the night after she was here. Miss Needlepoint thinks it was a scandal no one did anything to help. Someone must have known she had nowhere to sleep, and whoever did is to blame for what's happened now.'

'Miss Wellcome's very ill but she's being well looked after,' their mother assured them after they had told her about the night she had spent in the waiting-room. 'You mustn't feel miserable. If she didn't want anyone to know about her troubles you couldn't have done any

more. Now directly she's well enough the almoner at the hospital will arrange for her to go to an old people's home.'

'But that's not what she wanted,' Rory told his sisters. 'She's always had a place of her own.'

Miss Wellcome seemed caught inside the big hospital. She was surrounded by grown-up people. The children sent flowers but she was too ill for them to visit her.

Rory was surprised to find that Miss Needlepoint understood how Miss Wellcome would feel far better than the others. Discussing her problems the receptionist banged the keys of her typewriter and bright spots of colour shone in her cheeks. One day when the rest of the family were out Rory lingered in her office long after he had received the latest report from the hospital.

'Being as comfortable as can be expected isn't getting better,' he said as he made a chain with the paper clips. 'That night in the waiting-room she did have a cough and she must have felt shivery or she wouldn't have wanted a hot-water bottle when it was so warm. We ought to have noticed and made her see a doctor.'

'Even your father didn't realize anything was amiss when he saw her the next day,' Miss Needlepoint told him. 'Living as she was, something was bound to happen sooner or later. If anyone's to blame it's Mrs Clarence for letting her leave the guest-house without making sure she had somewhere else to go. There's such a thing as a sense of responsibility.'

Miss Needlepoint paused to answer the telephone and then turned to Rory with a smile.

'I'm sure you'll find that Miss Wellcome is much better soon. When she is you can take this along to her. She left it in the waiting-room after her appointment.'

From the stationery cupboard Miss Needlepoint took a worn suede shopping bag full of papers and handed it to Rory before going on with her work.

'Miss Needlepoint doesn't think anything in the bag is of much value,' Rory told Porterhouse when he showed him the shopping bag, 'but she thought she might like to have it.'

'But those papers are the poems which Miss Wellcome was writing when I sat by her in the summerhouse,' said Porterhouse looking far more cheerful than he had for several days. 'Once they were made into a book Miss Wellcome used to say all her problems might be solved.'

Rory stared at the verses written on the backs of Christmas cards, the lined guide-sheets from notepaper pads, tinted pages torn from an autograph album, the back of a notice about the summer storage of fur coats, an income tax form for the financial year 1945 to 1946, and a sheaf of notepaper samples.

'If Miss Wellcome wanted her poems made into a book that's what we must do,' said Rory.

'Would you and your sisters know how to go about it?' asked Porterhouse hopefully.

Staring at the papers spread out on the play-room floor Rory paused.

'I shan't ask the others,' he said. 'We'll manage it alone.'

9 The Old Firm

During the next two weeks everyone in the dentist's house was extra busy. Miss Needlepoint was on holiday. Their mother took over the receptionist's work as well as preparing her new autumn lectures on flibbertigibbets, bogles, hob-goblins and banshees.

Mr Cooper's appointment book bristled with entries. He scarcely stopped work between breakfast and supper. Most of his extra patients were holiday makers in need of emergency treatment.

'It's that peppermint rock which does the damage,' he explained to his family. 'If I've replaced one filling this week I've replaced a dozen. "The dentist's friend," old Mr Prince used to call it. He always reckoned to pay his boy's school fees for the Christmas term entirely from the fees for the extra work peppermint rock caused him in the summer holidays.'

In hospital Miss Wellcome made slow progress. Once Joy and Felicity visited her but Rory chose to stay at home with Porterhouse.

'You could easily have come,' Felicity told him on their return. 'Miss Wellcome didn't even look really ill – only much smaller, and her hair was very straight because the nurse had washed and cut it for her and she couldn't use her curling tongs in bed. Mummy's arranged with the Matron for her hairdresser to go in and set it for her.'

'And all the nurses loved that photograph of Porterhouse we sent,' said Joy. 'She keeps it on the locker right by her bed in a silver frame. She put the photograph over one of a great-aunt she never really cared for.'

'Just as we were leaving, Miss Wellcome said she thought she'd left her bag full of papers in the waiting-room,' said Felicity. 'We weren't to bother to take them specially, because she doesn't think they're likely to be of much real value, but she'll fetch them when she's better. We told Mummy, and she says she's sure Miss Needlepoint put them away in the office.'

Rory was silent. He couldn't explain that he didn't want to see Miss Wellcome until he had succeeded in making her poems into a book.

'Sending the manuscript to that publisher in London was just a waste of time,' Rory remarked to Porterhouse, 'even if they did print that book of poems we have at school. Miss Wellcome's poems are miles better, but most of them had never even been taken out of the shopping bag. That one about a field mouse on the income tax form was crumpled at the bottom when they came back. What we need to find is a publisher much nearer, where we can take the poems ourselves and make certain they're read.'

Rory found what he was seeking that night when his father drove him to Miss Needlepoints' flat with some documents that he wanted her to study when she returned the next day. Just after they left the flat as Rory looked from the car window at the busy street he noticed a shop with a red electric sign.

'"F. Honesty, Bookmaker," was what it said,' he told Porterhouse the moment he reached home, 'and underneath in green "Honesty's the Name and Honesty's Our Policy!" It's at the far end of the town but a bus goes all the way and we can easily get there.'

Joy and Felicity set out for the swimming baths the next day soon after lunch.

'You might come and be a body for our lifesaving,' urged Felicity, but Rory refused. With the shopping bag under his arm and Porterhouse beside him he hurried towards the bus stop.

On the top deck of the omnibus they shared the front seat with a large woman wearing purple beach slacks, a spotted orange sun-top and a fringed sun-hat. With a surf board, a rolled canvas wind-shield, and a beach ball, there was little room for Porterhouse, and he sat in the aisle.

'Taking your pussy to the Vet then?' she asked, smiling kindly, and Rory told her he wasn't. Afterwards she twisted round to point out Porterhouse to her children seated two rows behind.

'That's something like a cat, that is,' she said and gave Porterhouse the remainder of a large extra special Cornish ice cream.

Porterhouse had barely washed the last drop from his whiskers when Rory hurried him off the bus.

'That's the place,' said Rory when they finally stood on the pavement, 'between the pet food shop and the fish-and-chips. The Bookmaker sign is made from one tube of red glass with water bubbling through it all the time.'

They hesitated outside the office. The lower half of the window was made of dark glass. All that was visible above was a prickly pear cactus, an oil painting of three race horses galloping neck and neck past the winning post, and a silver cardboard horseshoe with a card which read 'To Fred, the Best in the Business, from a grateful client.'

'That shows the authors like him,' said Rory. 'He sounds quite different from that editor in London who sent back Miss Wellcome's poem with that slip saying he regretted they were unsuitable for his requirements. If Mr Honesty's so fond of horses he's sure to enjoy making Miss Wellcome's poems into a book. Heaps of them are about animals.'

The main door was shut, but Mr Honesty's visiting card was pinned beside a bell on a side door with a pencilled note advising callers to ring twice and walk straight up.

The staircase was dimly lit. It smelt of car ashtrays and kippers.

They blinked as a door on the landing opened and a large man in a checked waistcoat peered down at them.

'Sorry,' he said, 'it's struck two and no bets can be laid after the first race.'

'It's not about a bet that we've come,' said Rory, 'but

a book that needs to be published. The lady who wrote it is in hospital now and it's still in bits, but the sign said you were a bookmaker and we think Miss Wellcome will get quite better directly we can tell her it's all arranged.'

Mr Honesty stared at Rory and the cat. Porterhouse rubbed his head against the rough tweed of the bookmaker's trousers and he bent to stroke his ear.

'Writing the poems was the only way Miss Wellcome thought she might earn enough money to pay for somewhere to live,' added Rory, 'and if you're fond of horses you're bound to like them. One poem about the donkey who pulled the lawn mower on the croquet lawn at their rectory goes on for pages and pages and it all rhymes.'

Mr Honesty mopped his brow with a large handkerchief patterned with horseshoes. Porterhouse's glowing eyes never shifted from his face and he went on purring all the time.

'I won't say I haven't as good an ear for a rhyme as the next man,' he said. 'When I was no more than a little lad I had the whole of *"Up the airy mountain"* off by heart and the best part of *"Once more into the breach, dear friends"* – but you'd best both step inside.'

Mr Honesty's sitting-room overlooked the street. The red electric sign just outside the window cast a rosy glow over the room. In one corner race horses galloped on an extra large television screen. The sound was turned down but the horses went on galloping all the time. On the walls hung photographs of horses and jockeys and

men in grey top hats with carnations in their buttonholes and smiling faces.

'Those must be some of the authors,' whispered Rory as Mr Honesty cleared a pair of binoculars and a shooting stick aside for Porterhouse to sit on the broad window-sill. 'They must be fearfully rich. One's written "Here's to the old firm" right across a real five-pound note.'

The room was full of interesting objects. A real rose-tinted fountain played in the centre of the table. Inside a carriage clock on the mantelshelf tiny riders sped round and round at full gallop – but not a book was in sight.

'Now,' said Mr Honesty when they were all settled, 'I'll be perfectly straight with you. Bookmaker I may be called – but books aren't rightly my business. That's horse racing. When folk want to risk their money backing a horse to win a race it's me they come to. I take their bets. If the horse they fancy loses I keep their money and if it wins I pay out according to the odds.'

Rory set the bag of poems down at his feet. Porterhouse stared intently out of the window as if the British railway delivery van and the lorry full of cement blocks in the street outside were of the utmost interest to him.

'It's a mistake anyone might make,' said Mr Honesty, 'and I'm proud to have been taken for a literary man. Given the time and your opportunities for book learning there's nothing I would have liked better.'

Miss Needlepoint felt rested after her holiday. In barely a fortnight her coach tour had visited six capitals in Europe. She was looking forward to recounting her adventures to her friend at the oculist's, who had gone no further than a guest-house owned by a great aunt at Hove.

As Miss Needlepoint re-stocked her larder from the shops near her flat she felt glad to be home and about to begin her work the following day. Even Porterhouse seemed less disturbing. No doubt he was a trifle large but with give and take they should be able to share the same house perfectly well. Miss Needlepoint was ready to let bygones be bygones. She meant to make a new start. In her suitcase at home, carefully wrapped in the brushed nylon petticoat she had taken in case the weather should turn chilly, was a new china bowl marked 'Du lait pour le chat' : 'Milk for the cat'. Beribboned French kittens tumbled round the sides. The girl in the shop had found an extra large size.

Miss Needlepoint was still thinking about Porterhouse as she studied the contents of the pet food shop window. What a really splendid purr the great cat had. She almost fancied she was able to hear it now above the noise of the traffic like the contented hum from a hive full of bees. Suddenly the sound of voices made her glance up. Stretched on the window-sill behind the sign above the bookmaker's shop lay Porterhouse, with a plastic washing-up bowl at his side and his whiskers still sticky with condensed milk. Smiling behind him stood Rory and, even as Miss Needlepoint watched, a large fat man in a bright checked waistcoat handed him three five-pound notes.

10 Moderation in All Things

'You can't blame Daddy for being a bit upset,' Felicity told Rory. 'When Miss Needlepoint 'phoned, the Rector was in the chair waiting for a stopping in his front tooth to harden. He heard almost everything, because Daddy was so puzzled that you should be in the betting shop at all he repeated most of what she told him twice to make sure it was right.'

'It meant Daddy had to cancel all the rest of his appointments just to fetch you and Porterhouse home,' added Joy. 'Miss Needlepoint wouldn't even go into the bookmaker's without him.'

'She was more upset than the Rector really,' said Felicity. 'She said she would never have dreamt that she should have seen you in such a den of iniquity, and with Porterhouse with you as well, just as if it was your ordinary home.'

'The Rector did his best to cheer Daddy up,' said Joy. 'He thought Porterhouse being there was a hopeful sign. It showed that you weren't really hardened and still had some affection for one of our dumb creatures. He said that even now if you were stopped at once, gambling might still not gain a real hold on you.'

'And he thought that winning such a glittering sum

straight off must have dazzled your eyes to the real danger of the path you had taken,' said Felicity. 'He went on thinking of more and more things to say all the time Daddy was backing the car out of the garage.'

'The Rector's going to say lots of them in his sermon next Sunday,' said Joy. 'It will be all about the dangers of gambling, especially to the young, but he's promised not to use your name. He'll only say "my young friend" or "a certain little lad in this parish". Hardly anyone will know he means you.'

Rory scowled. He knew the twins only meant to tease him but he was still disappointed and cross with himself about the mistake he had made.

'Anyone but Miss Needlepoint would have guessed those five-pound notes the bookmaker handed me wasn't money I'd won on a horse race. If Mr Honesty wanted to pay five pounds each for three of Miss Wellcome's poems to hang over his mantelpiece it wasn't anyone's business but his. He chose the verses written on pink paper edged with gold from an old autograph album and they'll look really good framed in weathered oak. He really minded about Miss Wellcome, and his firm isn't a den of anything. It's one of the best spoken of on the turf. "If folk want to make mugs of themselves," he said, "they could do worse than come to me." But he was pleased to be mistaken for a publisher, and given the book-learning, he said, that's what he would have liked to be.'

Miss Wellcome herself was touched by the bookmaker's kindness but she refused to accept the money.

'She's written to him to say that she'll be delighted if he'll keep the poems,' Mrs Cooper told Rory. 'She's proud that he should want to frame them but she really wouldn't feel entitled to taking any payment for them.'

'Then I might just as well not have bothered,' said Rory with a sniff. Mrs Cooper smiled at his cast-down face.

'Now for goodness' sake cheer up,' she said. 'Miss Wellcome sent you her love and she asked me particularly to thank you for what you tried to do. It's given her fresh heart to try to place the poems herself one day. Directly she's settled in her new home she'll go through them, and Miss Needlepoint will type them for her. Then at least they can be submitted to some magazines.'

In spite of her words Rory still seemed gloomy. Even the twins noticed his worried frown.

'It's Porterhouse he's worrying about,' said Felicity. 'Once he was pleased because he's so much bigger than other cats, but yesterday when I said Porterhouse was so wide there wasn't room for anyone to pass him on the stairs Rory just glared.'

Porterhouse did seem much larger. Patients blinked when they met him in the hall. Even their toothache was forgotten as they stared after him moving silently down the passage.

Porterhouse himself seemed uneasy. Once he asked the children if their father had ever considered moving into a bigger house.

'Of course not,' said Rory. 'Daddy will stay here till he's really old and wants to retire.'

'It was only a thought,' said Porterhouse. 'Some of the rooms do seem a trifle cramped with hardly space enough to swing a cat.'

'To swing you we'd need the Albert Hall,' said Felicity as Porterhouse's tail rocked two favourite ornaments of their mother's on the mantelpiece.

'You shouldn't have said that,' Joy told her afterwards. 'Porterhouse looked really hurt.'

They knew something would have to be done. None of them guessed it would be Porterhouse who would do it.

'Porterhouse has gone,' Rory told his sisters early one morning in September. 'He's not in the garden or next door. He's just disappeared.'

The house was empty and tidy. No paw marks patterned the kitchen tiles, and the cat's milk bowl stood empty by the refrigerator. Even the cushion on his bed was unrumpled. Outside it was raining. Mist covered the valley. They thought of omnibuses and lorries thundering along the main roads and the big cat walking alone.

'He can't have gone far,' said their father, 'and someone's bound to have seen him.'

They all searched. Mrs Cooper took the car. The girls and Rory went on foot and their father rode his racing bicycle. His oilskins shone sun-gold as he sped along.

'Daddy found Porterhouse before,' Felicity reminded Rory as they hurried down the alleyway at the foot of their garden. 'Probably he'll be just as lucky again.'

'Not if Porterhouse doesn't want to be found,' said Rory gloomily. 'He's minded about being so large for ages now. He won't even let me weigh him any more, and he walked straight out of the room when they sang the wider still and wider bit from "Land Of Hope And Glory" at the last promenade concert on the television.'

They trailed miserably home at nine. Their bare toes were pale and wrinkled inside their sodden sandals and raincoats flapped round their knees. Their voices were hoarse from calling the lost cat.

Rory smelt the scent of a cod's head that had boiled over as they opened the front door. Even before their mother spoke they guessed that all was well.

'That nice policeman who came about the guest-house salmon brought Porterhouse back half an hour ago,' she told them. 'He found him just plodding along the main road well out of the town.'

'They sent him home in a Black Maria,' said Mr Cooper proudly. 'It caused quite a sensation.'

Porterhouse ate the cod's head, eyes and all, at breakfast, with a bowl full of porridge and his favourite condensed milk. His damp fur steamed in the warmth of the electric fire. He purred softly as the family finished their own breakfast but didn't meet the children's eyes.

'Of course it was nothing any of you had said,' Porterhouse assured them when they were alone in the playroom. 'No one could have made me more welcome, but I saw myself that I was causing you all real embarrassment. Even some of your father's patients have already gone elsewhere.'

'Only Mrs Clarence,' said Felicity, 'and that lady from the tea shop who says all cats make her sneeze.'

'And it wasn't really because of you that the girl from the cash desk at the cinema had hysterics,' said Joy. 'She always makes a fuss. Just bumping into her as you ran down the stairs can't have made all that difference.'

Porterhouse looked at them all fondly. They guessed he knew they were only trying to cheer him up.

'It's my size that's wrong,' he said. 'No one can deny – it just doesn't suit.'

'Then that's my fault, not yours,' said Rory, 'and however difficult it is you're not going to leave us.'

'And if that policeman hadn't found you I don't see where you would have gone,' said Felicity. 'Most cats' homes are always full up without having to find room for anyone as large as you.'

'I thought possibly a zoo,' said Porterhouse quietly. 'I should not have felt out of place in one of the larger cat houses.'

They left Porterhouse asleep on the sofa. Downstairs only Miss Needlepoint was in the house. Their mother had set out to deliver the first of her autumn lectures on 'Hobgoblins and Foul Fiends' to a Senior Citizens' Club thirty miles away, and their father was at the hospital. It was still raining.

'Mummy meant us to go for a picnic,' said Felicity. 'She's left one all packed on the kitchen table, and money for our bus fares if we want to take a bus out into the country.'

'It's the last one we'll have before we go back to school,' said Joy, 'and the rain can't go on all day.'

'You go,' said Rory. 'I'll stay with Porterhouse.'

'I suppose we might just eat the picnic here,' said Felicity, 'and we could wash our hair. It's still damp from the rain anyway.'

Miss Needlepoint found Rory alone in the waiting-room when she hurried in ten minutes later.

'A letter's come for Miss Wellcome,' she told him. 'How it came to be addressed to her here I can't imagine, but I thought you might run round to the hospital with it. It seems to be only a circular about some cat food or other, but she may like to have it before she moves to the Old People's Home tomorrow.'

Rory took the letter and stuffed it into his pocket without looking up from the *Geographical Magazine* which he was reading. He sniffed and Miss Needlepoint hesitated in the doorway. She remembered the bleak afternoon in January when Rory had once before been left in her charge. For months now she had tried not to believe that anything Rory had done then was linked with the arrival of Porterhouse and his extraordinary size. Now that Rory looked so miserable she was ready for his sake to face facts.

'If you're worried about Porterhouse,' she said, 'and feel responsible I hope you'll remember that a trouble shared is a trouble halved.'

Rory looked up. Suddenly he knew that talking to Miss Needlepoint about Porterhouse would be easier than talking about him to anyone else, because she had been there from the beginning. Seated at the table Miss Needlepoint listened to all he told her about the spell he had worked with the skull called Simonsbath, as calmly as she would have listened to a patient's account of pain from a troublesome tooth.

'At first when the spell worked so well I was pleased,' said Rory. 'Porterhouse is the best cat anyone could have, but now he's so huge we just don't know what to do.'

Miss Needlepoint straightened the magazines on the table.

'It's perfectly simple,' she said. 'You must end this business as you began.'

'But how?' asked Rory.

'It's unfortunate, of course,' said Miss Needlepoint as if she was advising the removal of a faulty tooth, 'but I can see no other course. You must dispose of the cause of your troubles.'

Rory stared.

'If you mean Porterhouse – we'd never part with him whatever happens.'

'Of course I don't mean your cat,' said Miss Needlepoint. 'That giant's skull is what's caused the bother. Once it's back where it belongs in the river at Simonsbath I fancy you'll have no further trouble.'

Miss Needlepoint looked up their route to the small Exmoor village which was two hours' bus ride from their seaside town. She packed the skull called Simonsbath in a cherry punnet well wrapped round with newspaper. The twins carried their picnic lunch.

'I've phoned our dental supply firm for a replacement,' Miss Needlepoint explained as she handed the punnet basket to Rory. 'You can pay me back the cost any time out of your pocket money. It will be far better for us to have a skull of a more usual size, and I very much doubt if your father will notice the change.'

Porterhouse stayed at home. He lay stretched out along the full length of the sofa.

'It will be all right,' Rory told him. 'Nothing will seem any different to you inside. You'll just shrink to an ordinary useful size.'

'Miss Needlepoint thinks you won't feel a thing,' added Joy. 'She'd never say that unless she was sure.'

'Of course not,' said Porterhouse sleepily as he rubbed the whiskered side of his jaw against Rory's wrist. 'No one could be more capable than Miss Needlepoint of taking the matter in hand.'

Rory remembered the letter Miss Needlepoint had given him for Miss Wellcome just as they boarded the bus.

'I'll take it on our way home,' he told the others. 'She's not leaving till tomorrow so that will be just as good.'

The sun was out and the rain had stopped when their bus set them down near the stone bridge at Simonsbath. The shallow river flowed between folded hills. After their journey they felt as if they had been tossed down into a pool of quietness. Under beech trees sheep cropped the short turf. A field below the small church was scattered with giant white rocks.

'Ought we to ask which is the right place?' Felicity

suggested as they stood on the bridge staring at the water far below.

'We can't,' said Rory with the cherry punnet clutched in his arms. 'If we did we should have to explain what we wanted to do.'

No one was about as they followed the footpath beside the river. Rain clouds crested the hills, and only the horned sheep looked up as they passed. Their footsteps were silent on the rainsodden grass.

'We'd better do it before we stop for lunch,' said Felicity.

The river deepened into a pool where the peaty water slid below humped rocks. In the freckled shallows trout swam barely visible in the sunlit water. They knew it was the place.

Rory lifted the skull from the punnet. The label had come unglued and curled from the base. The copperplate writing was faded in the bright sun. The sockets of the skull were dusty. It was still scented with the antiseptic used in their father's surgery.

Rory felt the sun warm on the smooth bone as he held the skull over the water. Then, as his sisters watched, he dropped it into the deep pool. For a moment the skull floated, then as the water flooded the dark caverns of its eyes it sank and the water closed over it. Only a dragonfly hovered above the rock where they knelt. The river flowed clean and cold towards the sea.

Travelling home on the bus Rory felt sick.

'You won't be,' said Felicity firmly. 'It's just that so much has happened you feel upside down.'

Rory didn't answer. He sat with his eyes fixed on the heather-covered hills and dry-stone walls. Nothing he had tried to do had worked out really well. Inside he still felt small. When they finally reached Pebblesea and scrambled off the bus it was Felicity who remembered the letter for Miss Wellcome.

'You wait with Joy and I'll run in with it,' she said as they paused outside the hospital. 'Probably she'll like to say "good-bye" before she goes tomorrow.'

Felicity was gone for a long time. Waiting with the picnic basket and all their mackintoshes on the crowded pavement Rory and Joy hardly spoke. Both of them were impatient to be home and to see what had happened to Porterhouse.

'If he's still the same and putting Simonsbath back hasn't worked what shall we do?' asked Joy.

But her brother didn't answer. His eyes were fixed on Felicity and their father racing towards them across the hospital courtyard.

'It's that letter,' said Felicity. 'It wasn't just a circular from the cat food firm, but the results of their competition. You sent in an entry from Miss Wellcome that she did the night she stayed in our waiting-room and it's won her the fully-furnished bungalow with oil fired central heating ...'

'And cat food for a year,' added their father, 'which she's promised to pass on to us for Porterhouse.'

Going home none of them felt tired any more. Their father rode beside them with most of their luggage piled on his bicycle. As they turned down their own crescent

Rory ran ahead. Beside the railings of their house, under their father's engraved brass plate, sat a medium sized tabby cat contentedly washing his snow white paws in the evening sunshine.

As the cat rubbed his head against Rory's scarred knees their father paused to stare.

'Either that cat's shrunk or Rory's grown,' he said with a smile and with Porterhouse bounding before them they went into the house.

Some other Puffins you might enjoy

Night Birds on Nantucket

Joan Aiken

Many years ago, late in the middle watch of a calm winter's night, a square-rigged three masted ship, the *Sarah Casket*, was making her way slowly through northern seas. And on the deck a child lay sleeping in a wooden box, so still and pale that she seemed more like a wax doll than a human being. It was Dido Twite, and she had been asleep for more than ten months. (Dido was missing, presumed dead at the end of *Black Hearts in Battersea*.)

This is Joan Aiken's third fantasy (the first was *The Wolves of Willoughby Chase*) and it is as deliciously outrageous as ever.

Horse in the House

William Corbin

Melanie Webb was one of those girls who can't live without a horse, and the one she had was a winner, a white palomino stallion called Orbit. He was never out of her thoughts, and he waited all day for the moment she came home from school to ride him.

Then Mom and Pop went off to San Francisco, giving Melanie a chance to put her cherished plan into action – her secret wish to bring Orbit inside the house.

The Witch's Daughter

Nina Bawden

Perdita is a witch's daughter and she is very unhappy living in a tumbledown house by the shore of a loch – until strange visitors lead her to hidden treasure, a mysterious secret, and her first real friendship.

An immensely readable story, by the author of *On the Run*.

The Exploits of Moominpappa

Tove Jansson

One cold and windy autumn evening many years ago a newspaper parcel was found on the doorstep of the Home for Moomin Foundlings. Inside the parcel lay poor shivering little Moominpappa (as he was later to become).

Then spring came, and Moominpappa decided to run away from the home and see what great events were awaiting him. And the friends who awaited him were people like Hodgkins of the hairy ears, the shy, jumpy Muddler, and Edward the colossal Booble, who was always trampling people underfoot and then conscientiously paying for their funerals. They were all rather eventful people, but the biggest event of all was when Moominpappa rescued a beautiful little Moomin woman from the waves, and discovered – Moominmamma.

The Rebels of Journey's End

Diana Frances Bell

Rufus wasn't the kind of mouse you would expect to see working in the headquarters of the mouse underworld, but he and his family had to live, and there was no honest work to be had. Because he had been buying up shops one by one, Joe Fingers had gained control of most of the Mousetown business, and it was very difficult for anyone honest to set up in business.

Then Joe Fingers ordered Rufus to kidnap a valuable cat and hold him hostage, and Rufus rebelled at last. With his friends Rikki the cat, Oscar the chipmunk, and a little girl called Donna, he set up an organization called the Rebels of Journey's End.

The Winter Princess

Mary Treadgold

Marilla was always cross on Fridays, because Friday was the day that Sara went to tea in Hampton Court, as a prize for a composition she had written about Africa.

And then Sara discovered that a real princess was coming to Hampton Court – an African princess, and they were going to meet her.

Application for membership of the Puffin Club

(Write clearly in block letters)

To: The Puffin Club Secretary,
Penguin Books Ltd,
Harmondsworth, Middlesex

I would like to join the Puffin Club. I enclose my membership fee for one year (see below) and would be glad if you would send me my badge and copy of *Puffin Post*.

Surname ....

Christian name(s) ....

Full Address ....

....

....

Age .... Date of Birth ....

School (name and address) ....

....

Where I buy my Puffins ....

Signature (optional) .... Date ....

Note: Membership fees for readers living in:
The U.K. or the Republic of Ireland 10s.
European countries 15s.
Elsewhere 25s.